LOST AND FOUND

FIVE STORY COLLECTION

DARA GIRARD

ILORI PRESS BOOKS, LLC

P.O. Box 10332

Silver Spring, MD 20914

www.iloripressbooks.com

Clifton Sisters

The Sapphire Pendant

The Amber Stone

The Emerald Ring

Fortune Brothers

A Tempting Proposal

A Seductive Arrangement

An Unforgettable Moment

CONTENTS

A THOUSAND WORDS

WRITING HAD BECOME PAINFUL, like a festering disease. Yvette couldn't understand why God would curse her with such an addiction--an addiction to write. She threw her notebook into the oversized vinyl bag, hanging over her shoulder and tried to smother the temptation as she gazed around the photo gallery with its pristine white walls, gray benches and carpeting. The serene order was a relief.

She had left her house in order to breathe, in order to escape her mind. Her one bedroom apartment, which was once a refuge, was now becoming a prison. Instead of seeing windows, she now saw bars; her door was a metal slab blocking her from the outside; the tassels of her rugs occasionally nipped at her heels as if trying to shackle her. The books on her shelves mocked her failure at acclaiming success as an author. Although she had published two volumes of short stories, reviewers had ignored them, readers had disregarded them and only a few booksellers still offered to display them. Even the hope of electronic distribution had not resurrected interest in her stories. Stories she had labored through now sat unread—it hurt, as if a baby she had given birth to had been left to die on top of a mountain.

But now she was out of the apartment and in the gallery of Pierre Dubois, a photographer who was quickly making his mark on the world. She had taken no notice of him or his work, but her friend had read about his gallery display in the newspaper and begged her to go. Unfortunately, at the last minute, her friend had bowed out of the arrangement, leaving Yvette to go alone. Since she needed the distraction she decided to come. So here she was, feeling like an outsider among the over dressed onlookers and magnificent artistry. But somehow it comforted her; no one paid attention to the dark skinned woman wearing a white blouse and cream colored pants, with a purple, silk scarf artistically draped over her shoulders. She didn't mind being a ghost. A nonbeing floating unnoticed in a realm of nothingness. No one tried to impress her. A story started to build itself in her mind about a woman who lived her life as a spirit, but she quickly brushed the thoughts aside, as if they were poisonous thoughts out to destroy her. Thinking of them as voices only a schizophrenic would hear and listen to.

She toyed with the scarf around her neck as she stared at a photograph titled: "Morning" with detached interest. Funny, she had titled a story "Morning" once. Not that it mattered. The photograph was of a flower covered in dew with the sun causing the dew to shine like molded crystals. It was painfully exquisite. She could feel her soul dying in its presence. The photographer had an eye, he had a talent that people were praising and she was glad for him, but it also tortured her, because she knew that the others in the gallery did not see what she saw.

She heard the words "compelling", "striking" and "innovative" bandied about like chocolate sprinkles on a cake, but those were shallow, hollow words that did not quite capture all that he was saying. She suddenly laughed at her foolishness—how could she possibly know what he meant anyway? She was only a writer—a dreamer, like him. Feeling suddenly weary, she sat down on a bench in front of a picture titled: "Anticipation". Yvette snorted. Another mockery of a story she had once written. It was a picture of a lake with the sun's rays fingering the waves as it descended behind distant mountains. She allowed herself to get lost in the picture, pushing people's voices into the background. Perhaps that's what she should do. She should find herself a lake and submerge herself in it. Cease existing. Cease torturing herself.

Again the desire to write rose up like a bonfire, burning her insides with the need to escape, but Yvette turned her heart cold, closing her eyes. Suddenly, a soothing female voice came over the loud speaker. "Ladies and gentlemen, please adjourn to Room 3B to see the unveiling of Chevalier's new piece, 'Acute Disparity', that will be auctioned."

The crowd murmured its delight; people emptied the main hall, like a room full of school children being let out for the holidays. Everyone left—except Yvette who sat motionless. The place was now as quiet as a library, only the barely audible buzzing of the lights could be heard overhead. She opened her eyes and stared at the picture, now seeing the reflection of her face in the glass.

"What do you think?" a deep voice asked from behind her.

She was not startled by its unexpected appearance. Few things startled her nowadays.

"It brings me sweet agony," she replied, not turning to the source of the voice.

The man paused. "Agony?"

She did not reply, not wanting to engage in conversation or explain her enigmatic response.

Undaunted, he sat down next to her, but far enough away to be non-threatening. Yvette observed him through the corner of her eye. He was a handsome man, his eyes were a lively brown and unusually kind—an expression she'd rarely seen in men with his physical attributes. His chin was solid with self-assurance, his nose poised but not haughty. Overall he had the kind of face seen in magazines, TV ads or movies. She looked down at his clothes— trousers made of fine wool and a blue shirt that complemented his brown skin. He looked out of place here, like Michelangelo's David in a toy store.

"How did you escape?" she asked suddenly.

He frowned, only enhancing his magnificent features. "What do you mean?"

She glanced over her shoulder. "The women. How did you escape them?"

He laughed. "Why do you ask? Because of my looks?"

Yvette sat back and again stared at the picture. It was

the laugh that had disappointed her—it was too knowing, too smug and just a little cynical. Perhaps she had misjudged him. Perhaps he was shaped more by his looks than she had assumed. He was no innocent Adonis.

He fell silent too for a moment and stared at the picture. "I hate that photograph," he said abruptly, violently.

She turned to him, her eyes silently asking him why.

"It's so deceptive," he replied. "Its beauty captured merely by the trick of the light, the right angle, the right lens."

He continued to talk and as he did Yvette was surprised that she hadn't listened to how beautiful his voice was. How pleasant she found the cadence of his words. She felt for him. How tiresome it must be to be so beautiful, to be perceived rather than understood.

"But—," she said, once he had finished. She paused, wanting to phrase her words properly. Not wanting to misunderstand the true meaning of his words. "All that you've said, do you think that's what the artist intended for you to see?"

He fell silent again. So silent that Yvette figured he hadn't heard her or just chose not to respond. Perhaps she had insulted him, she didn't care.

She looked at the photograph a bit longer—eyeing the waves and the sunlight dancing on the water. If she focused enough she could feel the breeze, see the water moving.

"You're wrong," she said suddenly surprised by the vehemence in her voice.

He looked at her startled. "Wrong?"

"The beauty was already there. It's not a trick of the light or shadow. It's not the right lens or the right angle. No one could be so arrogant as to believe such superficial things could create such beauty. The beauty was there to be captured."

"Ah, but the camera can make anything beautiful—a muddy beach, a swamp, a toad."

She flashed him a sly smirk. "And who is to say those things aren't beautiful?"

He shook his head, and a smile tugged at the corner of his mouth.

"The camera catches things we chose to ignore," she continued.

"Yes."

"It's a magnificent study," she said, an intrusive sadness crushing her chest. All of a sudden she felt worn and tired. In this one photo this man had accomplished more than she ever would with her stories—the dead babies she had labored over for years. She felt the photos laughing at her as her books had. They had the same names as her stories, didn't they? They taunted and teased her. How can you call yourself an artist? What have you done? Who knows you? Suddenly she felt the walls closing in on her. She shouldn't have come. She shouldn't have engaged in conversation with this handsome stranger who seemed to be studying her more than the photograph. She stood up wanting to be a ghost again, wanting to disappear into the walls.

"Where are you going?" the man said.

But Yvette raced out the doors, her scarf trailing behind her as if waving goodbye.

OH SUCH BRILLIANCE! Yvette thought as she cried, gulping the outside air, the sky heavy with dark clouds. It pained her to be in the presence of it. And she felt that she was the only one who truly knew the photographer's mind. But he received success while she sat on a cold pavement, contemplating what to do next. Should she continue to live and toil over words that would ultimately be unread? Words that would touch no one's life? Or should she become a ghost. A real one?

A bolt of lightning scared Yvette out of her morbid thoughts and lit up the sky like an explosion of fireworks. The sky opened up and the rain came down like giant bullets, hitting her shoulders and head with hard precision. Yvette jumped to her feet and ran for her car. It seemed she would remain human for another day.

At home she dried herself and thought about the handsome stranger whose eyes were too kind for his face. Eyes that must have seen a lot, but chose to be optimistic anyway. A man with his features should have had eyes full of arrogance, vanity, self-reliance, and not such a haunting intelligence.

Yvette paused, glancing down at the pen in her hand and the thoughts she had scribbled on a napkin. She tore the napkin up, letting it fall like confetti on the table. She would not write. She couldn't stand the pain. She would think of other things.

Unfortunately, her mind betrayed her and focused on nothing else but the stranger and the photograph. So deceptive, so beautiful, yet eerily familiar. Why?

She yawned, tired but resigned. She could not leave a question unanswered. She would visit the gallery again tomorrow.

SHE HADN'T EXPECTED to see the stranger there the next day, so she thought it an interesting coincidence when she bumped into him and spilled the contents of her purse on the floor.

He graciously bent down to help her, picking up her digital recorder and a notebook that had story ideas scribbled in it.

"Ah, that explains it," he said, handing her the notebook.

"Explains what?"

He nodded towards the notebook she was shoving to the bottom of her bag. "You're a writer."

"I used to be," she mumbled, retrieving the pens and pencils he was handing her.

"No. You're one of those born writers. Even if you physically stop writing, you'll be writing in your head."

"No, writing is an act. You must write to be a writer."

"True, but writing is also an occupation. How you see the world and live in it."

She found the thought thoroughly depressing.

"What do you write?" he asked, determined to address her as a writer, although she no longer wanted to see herself as one.

She stood, adjusting the bag on her shoulder. "What does it matter?" She turned and began to look around the gallery, trying to ignore the fact that the man shadowed her. After a few moments she asked, "Why are you following me?"

"Because I'm curious to hear what you think of my photographs."

She paused, but not from surprise, merely curiosity. "You're Pierre Dubois," she said, her tone flat.

"I was wondering if you would guess."

"It figures." He had been blessed with a face and a mind that people responded to. If the biography she had read about him--the picture of him conspicuously absent--had been correct he'd once been a model. While she with her ordinary features and passionate prose, went unnoticed and continued to do so. She suddenly felt envious of him. Envious of his joy and peace. "Your work is marvelous as you well know. So why do you ask me?" Just like the books and photographs had, she felt that he was in some way mocking her.

"I had help you know."

Yvette sat down and stared at a photograph titled: "Waiting for Freedom." It was a picture of a puppy waiting by a screen door for its master to return. She scowled. She had given that title to a story once. The coincidence only showed that words belonged to no one. No matter how lovingly she worked with them. They'd never be her own. Shakespeare owned his words, Emily Dickinson owned her words, bell hooks possessed her words—but she owned nothing.

She wasn't interested in who had helped him. She didn't care about him. She didn't care about anything. Before perhaps, but not now. Not when the blood running through her veins felt like they were congealing, leaving her body numb.

"Have you ever heard of Sandra Oni?" Pierre said undaunted by her silence.

Yvette's heart constricted painfully at the sound of the name. "Yes," she said, her voice rough, like a cat's tongue. She didn't wish to talk about her.

"I'm surprised. Few people have heard of her. She was my Muse. Still is in many ways. Her words touched me in such a manner that I knew I had to be what I was just in order to honor her prose."

"I don't believe you," she said, her voice low.

He cleared his throat and began to recite a quote. His melodious voice giving life to thoughts and feelings she had buried. " 'And then I saw myself, rushing, hoping, praying that my mind would not lead me astray into believing I was something I was not, something that was created rather than evolved.'"

For once Yvette felt something akin to surprise.

Pierre took her hand in his and stared intently into her face. His kindly brown eyes lighting a candle in her soul. "Why do you think I named my photographs after her stories?"

Yvette did not respond. Could not respond. Her heart was too full. To be recognized, to be acknowledged, felt so sweet. So the small picture--that she'd initially fought against--at the back of her books hadn't gone unnoticed.

"It's not about who you don't reach," he said. "It's about who you do. The pleasure I give to people now is due to the pleasure you gave to me and hopefully will continue to give in the future."

"But why—why do you like my work?" Yvette asked, eager to hear praise, eager to receive validation, eager to know that her work mattered.

"Because you spoke to my soul." He squeezed her hand. "Be patient. One day the beauty of your words will be known."

"And if it never is?" she asked, stating the true fear that had been haunting her.

He shrugged. "It still lives in the hearts of those who know it."

Yvette sighed. "So I must be content with being a ghost?"

Pierre glanced down at their interlocked fingers. "No, not a ghost. A kindred spirit waiting for flight." He kissed her hand, offering her promises she hoped he could keep. Again he looked into her face and this time he was rewarded with a smile so beautiful, so stunning that he caught his breath. He had more words to say, but he said them with his eyes instead and Yvette replied with her own. Then he left her, but Yvette knew that he would come back, when he felt she was ready for his presence. She could now feel the blood rushing through her veins. She could feel his lips on her hand, could enjoy the stories that occupied her thoughts and taste the joy in experiencing surprise and delight. She would no longer be a ghost. She could not dishonor her spirit that way, nor spirits like her. Yvette looked up at a passing woman and smiled, then took out her notebook and pen and began to write...

TEN DAYS OF GRACE

TEN DAYS OF GRACE

AND THE SNOW fell on the tiny casket, not as an ending but as a beginning. A beginning that started ten days ago.

It was ten days ago when Tessa Counton wrote her resignation letter. She'd written it five times over the last three weeks only to delete it and go to work. But this time was for real. She was tired of the internal politics, the lack of funds, and the parents who thought she could do more when she'd tried her best. When had nursing become a job instead of a passion? She remembered wanting to be a nurse all her life. At five she was bandaging up the family dog, and asking her sister, after she'd fallen off her bike, to tell her where it hurt. She became a candy striper in her teens and her conviction only grew. Nursing was her calling. It was when her sister's child was born premature that she knew the neonatal unit was her destination. Those babies called her.

Where had the passion gone? When had it become only about tubes and breathing monitors and grim news?

She was burnt out. Her husband said so and she was of no use to anyone. She pushed the button on her computer and printed the letter. She couldn't wait to hand in her resignation, to make it final.

But when her supervisor saw the envelope, he shook his head. "Put that away. I won't accept it."

"You have to. This is my two weeks' notice."

"Take a vacation, a holiday. This is what you were born to do. Just think about it."

She set the letter down. "I have."

She left his office feeling a sense of relief. Soon she wouldn't be here. She wouldn't see these hospital walls again, or have to deal with arrogant doctors and devastated parents. Maybe she'd volunteer or help with some cause, she needed to feel useful again. To know she was making a difference. She knew she'd be easily replaced. In this recession, many people were seeing the benefit of nursing. Then she met Grace.

She was beautiful--like a sleeping doll. Fully formed. She didn't look as if she belonged there. Then she saw her chart--No brain activity.

Tessa became Grace's guardian. Her parents had already agreed to disconnect any artificial life support. But Grace kept on breathing. For ten days, Tessa bathed, touched and talked to the baby and felt herself reborn. The memory of the many other babies she'd nursed over the years flooded her mind. Some had lived, others hadn't. She'd been on the journey with each one of them. It wasn't something that would be rewarded by applause or recognition, but she realized it wasn't about that. Grace would pass through this life unnoticed by most, but that didn't make her presence any less remarkable. And Tessa soon felt a new reason to press on.

———

IT WAS ten days ago when Luellen held her daughter in her arms, twenty-eight years seeming to melt away, as she held her little girl again. She held her dear child as her daughter wailed for the life she'd brought in and the one she would soon lose. Luellen held her child, fighting back her own tears, her own pain, which gripped her heart like a fist, cursing and praying and pleading all at the same time. Wanting it all to be a bad dream. Wanting to see her daughter and son-in-law take Grace home. The baby they'd been waiting for. But the nursery would remain empty.

Luellen held her child knowing there were no words to say, the pain had passed the salve of careless platitudes. She could already hear the words of some of her friends offering awkward comfort. "She's young, she can try for another," one would say.

"At least the baby's not in pain," another would say.

"At least she was able to conceive, there are other women who are barren," a third would add.

And she would hold down her simmering anger with a smile and try to be polite, even though she wanted to shout, "Allow us our misery! Don't force us to pretend it doesn't hurt because it makes you uncomfortable. Allow me my rage!"

But no, she would smile because just like now, as she held her daughter, she had no words. Because there were no words to say. Instead of a christening they'd be planning a funeral.

But as the days passed and Luellen rocked her daughter, smoothing back her hair, feeling the wetness of her tears on her arm, she remembered seeing Grace lying still in her cot. Grace was lovely as a rainbow with perfect features. Oh, how she loved her. And she wasn't ashamed of her love. She felt her heart shift, knowing she could and would love her daughter through this pain. A pain she thought would break her had somehow given her new sight. She saw her husband differently, loving him in a whole new way--the man she'd been married to for more than thirty years. He had kept her from crumbling, holding her in his arms, their tears mingling as their cheeks pressed together outside in the hospital hallway where their daughter could not see. He was her shield so that she could be their daughter's shelter. Because of Grace, she'd found a strength she didn't know she had.

IT WAS ten days ago when Dr. Wyner crushed her last cigarette of the day under her high heels and then got plastered because she could and didn't care. A week later, she lectured a group of residents about a sight she'd never seen before. It was like something from a freak show. She knew it was a harsh term, but it helped her to distance herself--making her feel like a spectator instead of a participant. But she couldn't pretend that it wasn't real. Grace was something she'd read and heard about, but never witnessed--a beautiful baby girl with no brain.

Well, yes the brain was there, but just as a holding object, like the stuffing in a teddy bear that gives it shape. The baby made her shiver in its beauty. How could it be so perfect in every other way but one?

It was disconcerting to see something so beautiful be so broken. She didn't like broken things. She didn't like unanswered questions, but now she had to face baby Grace. Grace who forced her to face her fears and her humanity. Dr. Wyner could no longer use her white coat as a wall. People looked at her with reverence and in the past she'd relished it. Relished the power and prestige of her white coat, the distinction and hierarchy it afforded her. She liked being looked at as the one with the answers. But now she didn't have them. There were no real answers to the many Whys that surrounded Grace. But the baby had taught her how to live with the uncertainty of questions, not to fight them.

AND THE SNOW continued to fall as the tiny casket went into the ground. Three women stared at the sight, completely changed by the last ten days of Grace. A baby who had barely lived, but had taught them how to.

DORCAS

DORCAS

Everybody knows that Dorcas Mortag burns everything she touches. If you want your house to still be standing you wouldn't let her set foot in your kitchen. She could burn water if given the chance. But she was never a bright woman—not thick mind you, just not brilliant. I don't say this to be mean. I say it because it's true. I found out how true it was when I made a foolish promise to her over forty years ago.

Secrets are hard to keep. I know. I've never been able to keep one, which is why people don't tell me things and I don't want them too. I have plenty of my own business in which to manage and I don't have time for someone else's mess cluttering up my mind. Promises are also hard to keep, but, unfortunately, easier to make. That's what got me into trouble. I'd made a simple promise a long time ago, never thinking much about it until I was asked to honor it.

It was little comfort that I wasn't the only one who'd

made this promise. We were three girls of twelve when we made our binding vow. I remember it was a rainy day in Port Antonio. My mother had gone to the shop and I was looking after my little sister when Dorcas, Aletta and Terry stopped by.

Dorcas wasn't much to look at, although she was best friends with her opposite, Terry, who had looks that had turned heads since the age of five and she had wealthy parents. Terry was cheery, small and kind. Dorcas was big and sweet. On the other hand, our friend, Aletta, had a face that looked like a truck had backed over it several times. People whispered that she'd come into the world crying and had never found a reason to smile. She was usually irritated or miserable, but she was clever and helped us with our homework, which was the main reason why we kept her in our circle.

They came to my house because I had the most space and adults were not usually around. My mother was always working. I didn't know where my father was--or to be honest *who* he was--and my uncle, who had a room down the hall, was always leaving some woman's bed before her husband showed up. That day, aside from the light patter of rain, I remember the smell of fish fritters and sorrel juice I'd made for my sister. Aletta sat and lit a cigarette.

I snatched it from her and stomped it out. "Yuh mad? You can't smoke here."

"Mi sorry," she said not sounding sorry at all.

I didn't let her attitude bother me as long as she didn't dare try to smoke again. My mother could smell the residue of anything—liquor taken from her cabinet, another woman's perfume on her boyfriend's shirt and *definitely* cigarette smoke in her prized sitting room.

"I want you to do something for me," Dorcas said. She had a sweet voice like pink candyfloss or an ice lolly. She could make you forget that sometimes what she said made no sense. "I want you to promise to lie for me."

"Why?" I asked.

Aletta scrunched up her face. "Lying is a sin."

"Not all lies," Dorcas said.

"Yes, they are." Aletta held her hand out. "Get me a bible and I'll prove it."

"She's right," I said. "Sometimes you have to lie."

"You should never lie."

I folded my arms and glanced at the bag where Aletta hid her cigarettes. "What do you tell your sister when her fags go missing?"

"I don't say anything."

"That's the same as lying."

"Why promise to lie for you?" Terry asked Dorcas before Aletta could challenge me.

Dorcas lowered her voice as if she were sharing a secret. "I want you to promise me, just in case I do something bad."

I laughed. "You'd never do anything bad." Out of the four of us, she was the least likely to get into any trouble.

"But just in case."

"I'll do it," Terry said.

I shrugged. "Me too."

We looked at Aletta.

She frowned. "What do we have to lie about?"

"I don't know yet," Dorcas said.

"All right."

Dorcas smiled and then her face grew serious and her gaze slowly went around the room as if assessing us. "You have to keep the lie or else."

Aletta sniffed. "Or else what?"

"You'll die."

She was a silly girl, but so were we and very dramatic back then. We'd read several English classics that told of undying loyalty and they added some adventure to our dull, ordinary lives. "We'll keep it," Terry said. Aletta and I nodded.

Dorcas' smile returned. Then she took out three marbles and held them in the palm of her hand. "I'll give one to each of you when I want the promise kept."

When I think of it now, I don't know whether to laugh or cry. How silly it was that we'd later do something so dangerous for a promise and a ritual of receiving a marble we'd discussed as children. I quickly forgot about it. I was sure all of us did. I was wrong.

AFTER THAT RAINY DAY, our thoughts turned to boys and dreams of leaving Jamaica. Well three of us dreamed about it, Aletta never did. She thought it was the height of foolishness and a waste of time. None of us saw her leaving and for years she didn't. She ended up working in town as a teacher at a private school. However, the rest of us did dream. Terry said a sailor would come and whisk her away. Instead she married a clerk who took her to England and she had two children.

Dorcas did once say she'd marry a man who'd take her off the island far away to England. And surprise, she did finally meet some man who'd said he'd take her. He was a good worker, simple, but kind and I've nothing against that. She was so happy, boasting how he was going to take her to Cambridge and how much she'd learn there. But the Cambridge to which he took her wasn't the one in England. It wasn't even close. It was in Massachusetts. Yes, he took her to America. She never did see England. None of us had thought of going to America, a place where they mangled the English language so much so sometimes one wasn't sure they were speaking English at all.

I married too. A man who took me off the island and settled us in Canada. I was lonely, I admit it, and the gray days settled heavy on my soul, but I loved my husband and our growing family.

Terry kept in touch with all of us. She was like the glue that tied us together. Her letters were always a welcome sight in the post box. She was so full of life, we didn't expect the cancer to take her so quickly. Her husband was unable to cope, and her parents were dead and none of her siblings wanted two extra mouths to feed, leaving her two little ones all alone. Dorcas offered to take them in, even though she'd been newly married. Lucky for her, her man didn't mind.

In the seventies, my husband's job took him to Virginia where I reconnected with Aletta. She'd married and divorced. She never mentioned her ex-husband and I never asked. Two years later Dorcas and her family moved to Maryland and we had a reunion. We gathered at my house because I still had the best food and the perfect space. I felt as if nothing had changed and half expected Terry to come through the door. And, for one brief moment, I thought she had when Deena, one of her daughters, came to greet me and then the other one, Lois. They both had their mother's beauty and kind, cheery nature.

Dorcas also had two little girls Michaela and Teresa—not pretty mind you—but sweet. She did dress all four girls as if they were princesses and doted on them. Her husband did too until him up and die on her only twenty-five years into the marriage. Fortunately, he left them enough money, which allowed the girls to educate themselves and find proper men to marry. Terry's two girls had no problem and both married right after college. It took another decade for Dorcas' eldest daughter to do so, but she did at last. Her younger daughter had a devil of time finding the right match (I even considered my own son for her, but my husband laughed at the idea). She was not only plain but shy, her mother prayed for a man to see her for who she was and she eventually did catch one. A fine looking man.

Aletta was sour, as usual, at the wedding. "I don't like him eyes," she said.

She always said strange things like that. "His eyes are fine," I said, wishing that Dorcas' daughter could have made a prettier bride.

"Then why him look 'pon the bridesmaids instead of the bride?"

I didn't know what to say. Michaela looked so happy and I was glad she was spared the lonely state of being single. A woman should marry. And if the man can be handsome that's good. "Don't make up stories."

"I'm not."

I ignored her and looked at Dorcas. She glowed. Six months later that glow was gone. I'd spotted her in a local shop and waved, but she looked right through me. I walked up to her and nudged her.

"Yuh not see mi wave?"

"Mi sorry I have troubles 'pon mi mind."

"What troubles?"

"Deena, is worried about Michaela and I haven't heard from her either. I have to see what's going on."

"How long has it been?"

"Two weeks."

"No need to worry."

"She calls me every week and we come here. Last time she told me she was sick and I asked if I could go see her and she said no. This time she didn't call."

"They're newly married. Perhaps she wants time alone."

"No, something's not right. That's not my daughter."

"She's a grown woman now."

Dorcas didn't listen to me. "Come with me."

———

MICHAELA LIVED in a lovely colonial house. Her new husband made a handsome income. It still surprised me that such a plain girl could have gotten herself a man who was both handsome and well off. But she was a good soul, so I was happy for her. What I didn't like was the garden, it was choked by weeds and I know Michaela wouldn't have allowed that to happen. Dorcas knocked. It was few moments before someone came to the door.

"Who is it?" Michaela asked.

"It's me darling," Dorcas said. "Your Mum."

Michaela seemed to hesitate then she opened the door.

I screamed first then her mother after me or it may have been the other way round, I'm not quite sure. But I do know that when I saw Michaela's face I let out a sound I didn't know I could make. I couldn't recognize her. And at that moment we knew that the fine looking man with a slow smile had a quick temper. He'd kept that temper well hidden. No one knew about it until that day.

Michaela looked around like a frightened mouse, pulled us inside and closed the door. "What do you want?"

"We wanted to see you."

"What happened?" I demanded.

Michaela lowered her gaze. "I was clumsy."

We knew that was a lie. She may look as dull as dishwater but she had the grace of a swan. "He did this to you?"

"He'll be home soon. You can't be here. Go."

"I can't leave you here."

"It will only make him angry. Please Mummy."

"No. Get your things."

"I can't leave him. He loves me. I just made him angry."

I stiffened with anger. "Your father never touched you and you let a man you lay with do this?"

Dorcas touched my sleeve to calm me. "You won't come with me?"

"No. It won't happen again."

"He promised you that?"

She nodded. Michaela froze when she heard a car door close. "He's home early. Don't say anything. Please."

I opened my mouth, but again Dorcas touched my sleeve, this time with more force. "We won't." She went into the living room and sat down, as if nothing had happened. That was how Michaela's husband found us when he came in carrying two dozen red roses and a gold necklace. I smiled at him and had to admit that Aletta had been right. I didn't like his eyes either.

———

A YEAR later Michaela gave her husband a son and four months after that he put her in the hospital with three fractured ribs, two black eyes and a broken nose. By that time it had become a family crisis. Dorcas' three daughters, Aletta and myself got together in the waiting room wondering what to do next.

"You see how he eats," Dorcas said. "That could work in our favor."

Aletta frowned. "How so?"

"A man like that can be poisoned."

Deena shook her head. "She wouldn't have the nerve."

"And it's against God," Aletta added.

Dorcas raised her voice. "Don't talk to me about God, when a man like that can be deacon in a church and not be struck down by lightning the moment he enters."

"There are other ways to get her away from him."

"She's too afraid. He said he'd kill her."

"She has to go to the police."

"Someone has to convince her."

"I will," Deena said.

And to my surprise she was able to persuade Michaela to press charges.

I held Dorcas' hand throughout the trial and Hudson's acquittal. Yes, the judge let him go because of his slow smile and charming ways. He said that hitting a woman was common where he came from and that he didn't know American ways and wouldn't do it again. He told lies about Michaela and made his actions seem justifiable. He walked out. Dorcas didn't move. But she began to smile.

"Yuh gone mad?" I asked her.

She only stood and turned to leave.

MICHAELA TRIED TO GET A DIVORCE, but Hudson wouldn't let her. He threatened to take full custody of their son.

Dorcas went through her savings, trying to help her daughter with her legal fees. But no matter how disappointing the defeat, Dorcas' smile never left her.

"She has me worried," I told Aletta one evening after Dorcas had left us. We'd just had tea together at Aletta's flat. We usually meet at my house, but for some reason my husband decided to catch a cold and stay home that week.

"It's that smile," Aletta said.

"You noticed it too?"

Aletta set her tea cup down with a clatter. "How can you miss it?"

"If you didn't know her, she just looked calm and happy."

"Yes, but we do know her," she said, her tone grave.

"What could it mean?"

"I don't know." Aletta sighed. "But she worried me with her talk about God."

"She was just angry."

Aletta shook her head. "And yet she smiles."

I thought about that smile all night and I thought about it even more the next week when Hudson went missing.

Dorcas came to my house and the smile was gone, but her candyfloss voice was pleasant. "If anybody asks. I was *not* with you and Aletta last Thursday."

I still remember the cool round feel of the marble as she placed it in my hand.

"DID YOU GET IT?" Aletta asked me that night, her voice tense.

"Yes. You?"

"You gone daft? Why would I be asking you if I hadn't?"

"We must do as she asked us," I said.

"It's not right. She was with us. Why should we lie?"

"We made a promise."

"We were children," Aletta countered.

"Doesn't matter."

"She won't change her mind. I've tried."

"What if we don't?"

"Do you want to risk it?"

I remembered Dorcas' words that we would die if we broke our promise. I didn't believe it, didn't want to, but an icy shiver of fear swept through me. "No."

Aletta sighed. "I wonder why she's asking us to do this now."

Two weeks later we found out. A body was found burned beyond recognition. Through dental records it was identified as Hudson. Dorcas confessed to the murder. She admitted to poisoning Hudson and then dumping his body and setting it alight. Naturally the police were skeptical. How could a woman of Dorcas' age and build have carried his body to a clearing and then torched it? However, no matter how long they questioned her, she didn't waver. The police were certain Michaela was somehow involved, but they could find no evidence to support their suspicions and she had a solid alibi--a broken wrist that Hudson had given her--that had sent her to the ER. Dorcas gave no other names and took full responsibility.

Michaela was just as distraught by her mother's confession, but there was an air of resignation when I visited her. Her plain little face was eerily composed. Her broken wrist in a sling. I helped care for her son and tidied up her place. When I glanced out the window I was surprised to see her garden was blooming. All the weeds were gone. I wondered how she had managed that after surviving such a severe beating.

Dorcas was indicted and later convicted. I remember the look between Deena and Dorcas and I thought of Michaela's garden and how the weeds were gone. I knew that Michaela couldn't have tended to the garden herself, and how as children Deena and Michaela had been so close, just as their mothers had been. Although they were not related by blood their souls, at times, seemed to be as one.

Although, I didn't want to, I imagined Deena being angered by Michaela's latest hospital visit and deciding to do something to stop him. I imagined her poisoning Hudson and then discarding the body somewhere. I imagined Deena telling her mother what had happened and Dorcas coming up with a plan. I imagined Dorcas burning his body. But of course, that's all just an old woman's conjecture. What could I know of such things? The truth could be vastly different.

The investigation is closed, but I know the truth: Dorcas was with us the night Hudson disappeared. But it's a secret I have to keep. I won't dare let it escape, even though I hate keeping it. Besides, it's not such a stretch to believe Dorcas' story. Everybody knows that Dorcas Mortag burns everything she touches.

THE PHONE CALL

THE PHONE CALL

"I BET you're a redhead with hazel eyes."

Regina Waters laughed. If the man on the phone reduced her credit card charge, she'd be whatever he wanted-- although she was tempted to say, 'I'm as dark as a roasted chestnut and just as hot'. She couldn't blame him for his inaccurate description. Her slight Welsh accent, that always became more pronounced when she was being polite, confused most people. The melodic cadence of her words always came as a shock when people first met her. She was a stately five foot nine with golden highlights in her black hair--not brunette, blonde or red--and she had eyes the color of coffee beans.

Back in school she'd gotten her head slammed into lockers for sounding white, for putting on airs. Most of the students in the DC public schools she'd attended, thought Wales was the plural form of a marine mammal. They'd never heard of the place, let alone black people living there.

In Wales, there had only been two other black families in the entire village. Even their nanny had been white. And most folks didn't want them there. They'd moved to another village which was a little more accommodating, but still isolating. Moving to the United States had been a dream for her. She admired the music, the food and the literature. She imagined going to a mixed school or one that was predominantly black, where she could blend in and not be a violet in a garden of daffodils. In America, she wouldn't have to guess whether the rosy cheeked teacher, who handed her back her exam with high marks and a smile, was truly proud of her efforts or just being patronizing.

The year her family arrived in their new homeland they faced a culture shock--the accents, the different manners--but Regina believed once she entered middle school she'd be accepted. Instead, the bullying had been doubly painful. She thought being in a majority black school would be a place where she'd finally belong. It would have been easier to endure if the bullying had been because of her height or her lack of athletic ability, she had no coordination. Even clapping on beat took considerable effort. But none of that had separated her from the other students. It was her accent. It alienated her, when before, the color of her skin had kept her apart.

"You have to fight back," her older sister had once said when thirteen year old Regina returned home missing an earring and sporting a massive bruise on her cheek. That day, one of her biggest tormentors, a big girl with hands the size of plates, had also taken her lunch money. Her older sister, by two years, was beautiful, fierce and her idol.

"I'm not very good at it," Regina said.

"I'll help you," her older brother said. He too had it rough, being just a year older than Regina, but managed to get through the school halls without incident. His large size was a benefit and he had a look that said 'Mess with me and I'll destroy you' along with an attitude he'd perfected years ago. The other students called him foul names, but they *never* touched him. For a week, her brother taught her fighting moves and her sister coached her from the sidelines. She was lanky and awkward, but determined. They lied to their West Indian parents about how their school days were going, knowing they'd never understand. They hadn't understood their children's lives in Wales--focusing solely on providing the basics of housing, clothing, food and education-- and wouldn't understand their lives in America either. That Tuesday, Regina got her head slammed into a locker, again, and her books knocked away, but this time she fought back.

And she lost.

She was pummeled to the ground, but not before leaving scars. Long, bloody scars and she was no longer afraid. No one ever bothered her again. By the time she entered college, she finally felt comfortable in her new homeland. She fell in easily with the international students and those who let her be herself, rather than complimenting her for being articulate or not sounding black. However, finding romance had been difficult.

Some men--lured in by her accent and background--

quickly became bored when they discovered she wasn't exotic enough. She liked hot pizza and cold beer, rock climbing and singing bawdy pub songs at the top of her voice, sometimes in Welsh. It was no surprise when her brother married a fair haired woman from Ireland--a woman who accepted her brother's shy ways, plaid shirts, beat-up car and obsession with Star Trek. Regina found a kindred spirit in her sister-in-law, who fit into their boisterous family.

But as the years passed, she wondered if she'd ever meet her match.

"Don't you feel rejected a little?" her friend Drea asked her as she and her other friend, Ann, took a lunch break from the architectural firm where they all worked. Drea was born and raised in Tennessee to Kenyan parents before moving East. Ann was a fourth generation Californian whose Asian American family couldn't believe she'd break with tradition and move to the East Coast. She'd met her at a college concert when Ann sat next to Regina and did a perfect imitation of a top British actress, impressing Regina with her ear for mimicry.

"Don't say it," Ann said.

"Say what?" Regina asked.

Drea sighed, clearly annoyed that Regina didn't understand. "Doesn't it bother you a little that your brother married a white woman?"

Regina paused, surprised by the question. She hadn't thought about it and wondered if she should have. "What does that have to do with me? Why would I feel rejected? I'm not marrying him." She shivered with disgust at the thought.

"Come on, another successful black man marrying white, you must see the trend."

"What trend?" Ann asked.

Drea waved her fork at her. "Sorry, but you wouldn't understand, you don't have that problem."

Ann rolled her eyes. "Oh, thanks."

"You're not being fair," Regina said in Ann's defense. "Remember that guy who had yellow fever and kept sending her love songs in Chinese, even though her family's ancestry is Japanese and Korean?"

"At least he thought she was desirable," Drea said.

"And we're not?"

"Not in the same way. Let's face the facts. Answer my question."

Regina frowned. "It's a silly question."

"Answer it anyway."

"Isn't the fact that we're here proof that black men like black women?"

"I didn't say *all*. I know there are exceptions but most prefer white or--" She sent Ann a significant look.

Ann held up her hand. "Don't even go there."

"No, I don't feel rejected," Regina said, knowing her friend wouldn't let the topic drop no matter how much she hated it. "I don't feel rejected or whatever else you said. She's perfect for him. Besides, the black girls gave him a hard time. They hardly looked at him."

Drea turned and watched a mixed couple sit down: A well dressed black man and his white companion. The two men sat and held hands, flashing matching wedding rings.

Drea's mouth fell open. "You see that?" she said in a loud whisper. "Damn, even the gay ones marry white!"

Regina shot a nervous glance in the couple's direction hoping they hadn't overheard. "Keep your voice down."

"Let's try a new topic," Ann said.

But Drea wouldn't let it die, the sight of the couple seeming to fuel her disgust. "Your sister is beautiful and she's not married yet. You know we're doomed."

Ann gently patted her friend on the shoulder. "Eat your food and be quiet."

Drea shrugged her hand away. "I'm serious about this."

"That's what scares me," Ann said.

Drea stared at Regina. "We're almost forty. Our time is running out."

"We're only thirty-three," Regina said, sending a confused look at Ann. Neither woman knew where their friend's sour outlook had come from. And they didn't know how to change it.

Drea played with her drinking straw and said in a sour tone. "It's easier for *them* anyway."

"I don't want to have this conversation," Regina said.

"Successful black men have their pick of partners," Drea said. "Successful black women don't. So, we either have to marry down or forget about marriage all together."

Ann folded her arms. "You're having man troubles, aren't you?"

"What do you mean?"

"This sudden tirade isn't coming from nowhere."

"It's not a tirade," Drea said annoyed.

"You haven't answered her question," Regina said.

"Trenton wants to move in."

Trenton was her boyfriend of six months. He worked in maintenance and changed jobs like most men changed shirts--casually and without thought. Neither Regina nor Ann ever had anything to say to him, both secretly finding him as interesting as a glob of tar. Regina once hinted that she thought Drea would be happier seeing someone more in her league, at least someone with similar interests, but Drea always ignored her.

"Do you blame him?" Ann said with a grin. "You've got a house and he's got his mother's basement."

"I told you he's only there to save money."

Ann raised a brow. "You still believe that?"

"What do you want?" Regina asked before her friends got into an argument.

Drea sat back and sighed. "I don't want to."

"Then don't."

"But I don't want to break up. I'd rather have someone than be alone. And there aren't many employed black man available."

"Stop with the statistics," Ann said. "It's not that bad."

"How would you know?" Drea snapped. "Survey any man and ask them what kind of woman they want and they'd chose a white woman first then an Asian woman. Black woman are always the last choice."

"That doesn't mean we still don't meet jerks or have bad relationships," Ann said.

"At least you--"

Regina held up her hands. "Wait, wait. Let's not fight about this. Drea, don't take your frustration out on Ann it's not her fault."

"I didn't say it was, but she shouldn't pretend that she has it as bad as we do."

"I wish you'd stop talking as if we're victims."

"We are. Victims of a society that doesn't value us. Everything has a price and our price is low."

"That's not true," Ann said.

Drea ignored her, keeping her gaze focused on Regina. "You're single and your sister is single and it's going to stay that way until you open your eyes and realize your options are limited."

Regina didn't want to believe that. She wanted to believe there was someone out there for her, someone who she could talk to, someone interesting, someone with whom she'd never run out of things to say. She didn't want to only see herself just through the eyes of a man. Wasn't she more than that? Wasn't that what women had fought--still fight--for--equality? Was her value only about how much she was desired? Wasn't there someone out there who could see how great she was?

But that night, after the credit card call, she started to doubt it. Most men wanted the long haired blonde or savvy brunette. They fell in love with their eyes and, to them, she would always be invisible.

SHE WAS CLEARING out her kitchen cupboards

when she ended up playing phone tag with her sister, who was helping her plan a fishing trip for their father for Father's Day. She finally got to talk to her when the phone suddenly disconnected. Seconds later it rang again and she answered.

"Don't put it there," she said, referring to the new fishing rod. "He'll know. It has to be put in a place he'll never guess. I can't wait to see his face when we take him to the lodge. A weekend fishing retreat will be so much fun for us." When her sister didn't reply she said, "Hello?" afraid she'd lost the connection again.

"Hello, I think I dialed the wrong number."

On the other line she heard the deepest, richest most beautiful voice she'd ever heard. As sweet as Georgia peaches, and hot as fudge with a slow, careful cadence. She hadn't thought much about Southern black men.

"Oh, I'm sorry," she said, ready to hang up.

"Never met a woman who enjoyed fishing," he said, before she disconnected.

"I don't. I just enjoy being out on the water in the quiet. Although, I don't think I gave you that impression just now, but I can sit silent for hours."

He laughed. "A woman who can just sit and say nothing? That's rare indeed."

"I'm rare in more ways than you can imagine."

For the next three hours, the two of them ended up talking about everything from the culinary value of beans on toast to the fate of the panda bear.

"I have to go," he said. "But I'd like to do this again."

Regina laughed. "Well, you have my number."

"Yes, but I don't know your name."

"It's Regina."

"I'm Benedict."

"Benedict? Really? I don't know any American Benedicts."

He laughed again. "I'm sure they're around. I was born in England and moved to the States when I was two."

She could feel her heart soar. Another connection. Perhaps a black man not born in the States could understand her background more. "Can I call you Benny for short?" she teased.

"No."

"I really like Benny Goodman."

"You cannot call me Benny."

She laughed. "How about Dic?"

"Absolutely not."

"Oh, well goodbye, *Benedict*."

"Bye, Regina."

She hung up the phone with a smile, not expecting him to call back, but glad she'd had a chance to speak to him. He made her feel beautiful. His voice conjuring thoughts of cold ocean waters on warm sand, candlelit dinners and crackling fires.

He called the next day. And then two days after that. Followed by five more calls and conversations that lasted for hours. Their conversations were intelligent, inventive, romantic. Sometimes the words didn't matter, even in the silences she felt a connection. She sensed a kinship. She spoke about her work and her recent trip to Portugal. He spoke about his work as an engineer and his trip to Turkey.

Regina listened to every detail. The sound of his voice at times like poetry--beautiful, at times enigmatic, at other times clear, but always enlightening, engaging and inspiring. His voice gave her a connection to the world when for so long she'd felt out of place. Regina floated through her days, looking forward to their almost daily talks until he said the unthinkable.

"I'd like to meet you," he said.

Regina swallowed, feeling her heart race. Through their talks they had discovered they lived in the same area, but she'd never thought of meeting him in person. "Why?"

"Why not?"

She bit her lip, searching her mind for excuses. *Why not? Because this relationship is perfect just the way it is. Because I don't want to ruin things. Because I don't want you to see me.*

"Regina? Are you still there?"

"Yes."

"How about dinner?"

Not coffee, not lunch. Dinner. Why did it have to be dinner? Dinner meant he was serious. Dinner meant he really wanted to get to know her. But didn't she also want to know him? She wanted to meet him too, right? But part of her was afraid--no terrified. Should she warn--tell--him that she was black? She loved talking to him and maybe since he was black and he'd travelled, he'd give her a chance. Maybe it wouldn't matter. Perhaps a successful black man would want to marry a successful black woman. He wouldn't care that she didn't fit the status symbol. Maybe he wouldn't be disappointed, but pleased.

She wouldn't let Drea's fears limit her. This could work. He wouldn't think she was putting on airs or trying to be someone else. He would accept the fact she wasn't a woman with creamy white skin and red blonde hair. "Okay."

They set a time to meet at a local restaurant that Saturday.

"How will I recognize you?" Benedict asked.

I'll be the tall black woman in a striped dress, she wanted to say, but then realized she was curious to meet him. She didn't want to give him a reason to change his mind. "I'll wear a hat with a red flower."

"And I'll carry a green rose."

"A green rose? I've never seen one before."

"They're not abundant in nature but very beautiful. You can't miss them."

SHE ONLY TOLD Ann about her date. Ann helped Regina select an outfit and walked with her to the restaurant.

"I wish I weren't so nervous," Regina said.

"You're going to be fine."

Regina smoothed back her hair. "I heard Drea's letting Trenton move in."

"And she's going to be miserable, but that's nothing new."

"Do you think--"

Ann shook her head. "Let's not talk about her right

now. You need to focus on your date with Benedict and your life, not hers."

"I'll give you a signal if I need help," Regina said walking into the crowed, busy waiting area of the restaurant.

She saw the rose first. An unusual color. Then she lifted her gaze to the man holding it. He was tall, good looking dressed in business casual attire. He was also all wrong. Her heart fell to the floor. "Oh no," she said then ducked behind a wall.

"What?" Ann asked. "Do you see him?" She made a face. "Is he gross? Don't you hate it when a guy has a great voice and looks like a--"

Regina shook her head. "No. It's not that. I can't see him." She tore off her hat. "I can't let him see me. I've got to go."

Ann grabbed her arm. "Why?"

"I thought he was *black*. How could I have been so wrong?"

"Where is he?" Ann demanded looking through the crowd.

Regina pointed to a man sitting at the bar. "He's not going to want to see me," she said starting to panic. "I shouldn't have said 'yes.' I should have told him that I was black over the phone, but I just wanted to see him. How could I be such an idiot? This is a disaster."

"It's not a disaster," Ann said taking the hat from her hand and placing it firmly back on her head.

"You're right. *You* should go out with him," she said shoving her foreword. "You'll like him."

"Are you crazy?" Ann said, her voice cracking in surprise. "I don't sound anything like you."

"You're great at mimicry. Remember how we met?"

"But--"

"Just for one night, please."

Ann shook her head. "I don't like this."

"Plus you look the part."

Ann narrowed her eyes. "Because I'm Asian and he's--"

Regina clasped her hands together in a plea. "Please do it for me, Ann. Please, he's checking his watch. I don't want him to think I stood him up."

Ann folded her arms unmoved. "But you are."

"Seeing you will soften the blow."

Ann frowned. "You've been listening to Drea too long. She's wrong about your options. You're funny, attractive and successful. Any guy would be lucky to have you. Give him a chance."

Regina wanted to believe her friend's words, thankful to have someone like her in her life, but fear still gripped her. "I don't want to see the disappointment on his face. I can't. I'll never ask you to do something like this again."

Ann glanced away and when she looked at Regina again, tears glistened in her eyes. " I really hated what Drea said to you the other day. I hated how she thought I didn't understand and most of all, I hated what she implied. Okay, so even if she's right and most men want a beautiful blonde, you don't need most men. You just need one. The right one. The one who loves you just the way you are. My grandmother once told me that true value is the price you put on yourself. I don't know if

Benedict is the right guy for you, but aren't you rejecting him too?"

"No, I--"

"Then go over there and say hi."

Regina hung her head, wishing she had the courage Ann had. Wishing fear didn't grip her so completely. "Okay, I admit I'm a coward. I can't see him."

Ann briefly squeezed her eyes shut then sighed dramatically. "Fine. I'll go meet him, but you wait here for my signal. Got it?"

Regina nodded, relieved. "Yes," she said, then watched Ann go over to Benedict, her feeling of relief quickly replaced by loss. It had all felt so perfect. Seemed so right, but it was just another illusion. Just like coming to America and thinking she'd fit in. She gripped her hands into fist, for a moment feeling like the thirteen year old who'd been bullied, whose wounds were still fresh, but she'd also fought back and although she'd lost, she'd won respect.

She thought of Ann's words. How much Ann cared for her. She was right. This was another battle, a battle against labels and others limitations. Love and self-respect were things to be claimed, not given. She had to respect herself, she had to believe that she was worthy, even if he didn't. She couldn't be afraid like Drea and think she deserved less, even if everyone else thought so. All that mattered was what she thought.

She'd always been an outsider looking in and never part of the crowd. She briefly closed her eyes and held back her tears. The signal hadn't come yet, so she'd give her friend another couple of minutes before she left.

She'd enjoy going fishing with her father. To be quiet. To stop dreaming.

She took a deep breath and walked over to them. She was strong enough to face whatever happened.

"She's really shy," she heard Ann say in her regular voice.

She paused, surprised that she wasn't trying to be her.

"I thought so," she heard Benedict say, then he looked up and their eyes met.

Ann turned around, flashing a proud grin and mouthed 'I knew you would come,' before she said, "It's about time you got here."

"Sorry for running late," Regina said.

Benedict handed her the rose. "I'm glad you could make it."

"Oh, thanks," she said taking the rose, finally letting it register that he didn't look disappointed, but he *did* look wary. Maybe he was hiding his feelings well. Maybe he was disappointed that Ann wasn't her.

"Would you like to join us?" she asked her friend.

"No, I'm leaving you two alone." She then leaned towards Regina and whispered, "You won't regret this," before saying goodbye to Benedict and leaving the two of them at the bar.

"Our table should be ready," he said.

"Right."

Minutes later they sat at the table with nothing to say.

Benedict sat back, shoved his hands into his pockets

and sighed. "Let me guess. I'm not what you were expecting."

No. His voice didn't match the good looking, six foot two, Asian American man who sat opposite her. The man who enjoyed extreme kayaking and rock music. The man whose calls she'd looked forward to for over a month.

And to her horror, her own assumptions and stereotypes loomed large in her mind, forcing her to face them with a sickening truth. Was it so bad that he wasn't black? "No," she said honestly, "but I bet I wasn't what your were expecting either."

"You're much prettier," he said. And she expected him to smile as if he'd made a joke, but he didn't.

She turned and pointed to a scar on her neck. "I got this from a girl who thought I was trying to sound white."

"I've got a couple scars of my own, but you can't see them until I get to know you much better."

"I hope I get a chance too."

He winked, then his face spread into a sexy grin. "You will."

Regina laughed and felt the tension between them disappear, they no longer had to pretend to be strangers. They no longer had to pretend to be someone else--they could be themselves. That night she said goodbye to the bullied thirteen year old. She no longer had to worry about fitting in or being the popular choice. The world was big and the options many. Ann was right, she didn't need most men to want her--just one. The right one.

The sights and sounds around her faded way as she dined and laughed and talked with the man sitting in front of her. She felt free to be a person, not a voice, or a race, just a woman and she felt giddy with the feeling of her new liberation. The evening ended faster than she'd hoped and soon they were saying goodbye in the parking lot--parting with a light kiss.

"I'll call you," he said, after walking her to her car.

She nodded then waved and watched him go. She lifted the green rose, inhaled its scent and smiled because she knew he would.

BERRY PICKING

ONE

DEAR GOD PLEASE *don't let that be him.* Paula Oyelowo offered this silent plea as she sat in a West Indian restaurant, Island Dining, watching a tall, dark man speak to the maître d' then walk towards her table. Except "walk" would be the wrong word. He bounded towards her through the elegant restaurant like the proverbial bull in a china shop. The men she usually went out with were more refined, like stallions. He was no stallion. His tie was crooked, one of the collars of his white shirt was up and the other down, his light gray tweed jacket had a dark smudge near the hem and he was vigorously wiping his hands with a paper towel--staining it black. Paula cringed. She'd been told he was an engineer, not a mechanic.

Paula forced a smile, but remained seated as she greeted her blind date, wishing, for the twentieth time, that she'd said no to the suggestion. But she'd promised her best friend, Tamara, that she'd try him out. Her friend had been insistent and over a six-month period, had bugged her every day until she said "yes." She had decided she would start to be mature when it came to relationships. She sighed. Being mature had meant going out with men who were a little older, in settled careers, and looking for marriage, but she had her standards and "first impressions" played a major role in her selection scheme. And she wasn't impressed. He was almost forty. Just in her age range since she'd hit the big 4-0 soon. In four years to be exact, but time seemed to be barreling towards her. It was time to get serious. To settle down.

"You're not getting younger, and before you know it, you'll be too old for any man to want," her mother liked to remind her. With a repetitiveness that bordered on the neurotic. Sure, she could still attract the under thirty set--especially those twenty-five to twenty-eight--but she hadn't had much luck with permanency. After two relationships that had ended badly she was willing to try something, or rather someone, new. But this date looked all wrong

"Sorry I'm late," he said in a rush, his accent a mix of a Northeastern region she couldn't place. At least he sounded sincere. "There was this lady with a flat tire." He collapsed into the chair in front of her then jumped up again as if on springs. "I haven't introduced myself." He held out his hand and promptly knocked over her water glass.

Paula leaped up in time so that the water only splashed her, rather than soaking her skirt. She bit back a swear word.

"Sorry about that," her date said, reaching for the

glass and hitting the flower in the center of the table with his elbow.

Paula grabbed the tiny crystal vase before it fell. "That's all right," she said. "Sit down. I'll handle it." Which she did by moving the vase off to her side of the table. She was used to handling crises. As a Management Consultant at a prestigious firm in Washington, D.C., she worked on merging the firm's clients with new partners to utilize and optimize their services. She was a genius at using technologies to provide greater opportunities for companies to form collaborations with others that advanced the decision-making capabilities of their organizations. It was a tough, high-profile position, and over the past seven years she had made a name for herself in the industry. Paula inwardly groaned, wondering why Tamara thought to set her up with such a clumsy man. One would think that by his age he would be able to manage his oversized hands and feet, instead of moving around like an awkward sixteen-year-old going through a growth spurt. He didn't need to introduce himself. She already knew the vital statistics. Name? Conrad Baynard. Age? Thirty-eight. Occupation? Mechanical engineer. Income? Six figures. Tamara had used that as one of his selling points as well as telling her he was one of the finest men she'd ever met.

He had a nice face. Not remarkable, but comfortable. Nothing to make her heart race or her skin tingle. To her he was like hot cinnamon chocolate--warm and sweet, but nothing more. She usually liked her men with a bit more spice. Paula sighed. It was going to be a long night.

She got the attention of a waiter. She had the table

changed, their settings rearranged with two new glasses of water. Then they ordered.

"Perhaps we should start over," Conrad said with a sheepish grin.

"No, let's just move ahead. You know my name and I know yours so we might as well get past the banal introductions and niceties to something more interesting."

He lifted a brow. "A woman who gets to the point?"

"I'm allergic to wasting time."

He nodded then fell silent.

She'd been too curt. That was a terrible habit of hers, but she really did hate wasting time. One of her greatest strengths was efficiency. She knew how to be productive. How to make things happen. But it seemed the date was DOA--dead on arrival. However, since she still had a meal to eat she needed to fill the time up with something. She'd never see him again so she decided she might as well make the most of it.

"So, tell me about yourself," Paula asked. Men usually liked to talk about themselves so she thought that would be a safe topic to begin with.

Conrad folded his arms and leaned back in his chair. "How much did she pay you?"

"Excuse me?"

"Tamara. Did she pay you to go out with me?"

"No," Paula stammered, feeling her face grow warm. She shifted in her chair annoyed. She never became flustered.

"Bribe you with something?" he asked, his gaze steady and intense.

"No." She tried to hold his gaze, but she had to briefly look away. "Why?"

"So you wanted to come?"

She returned her gaze to his. "Yes."

His eyes lightened with amusement and a grin spread on his face. "Then relax and stop acting like this is either the Inquisition or a job interview."

Paula stared at him for a moment then laughed, suddenly relieved. "It's that obvious?"

"If you glance at your watch one more time I'll start to feel like a lab rat."

"A lab rat?"

"An experiment."

Paula nodded and lowered her watch. "Sorry, this is my first blind date."

"Good. Me too. So there's no pressure. There's nothing to compare it to."

Except a non-blind date, but that didn't matter. Paula felt her tension ebb. "So what do you do for fun?"

"I play in a band."

"Really?" she said surprised. "What instrument?"

"The tuba."

She inwardly groaned. The tuba. Not a sexy instrument like the saxophone or piano, but a big bulky horn instrument. "Why?" she asked just to be polite. She wasn't really interested.

"By the fifth grade I was already as tall as my teacher and I wanted an instrument bigger than me, so it was a choice between the tuba or the cello. I chose the tuba because I liked how they looked in the marching band."

He chose an instrument only because it would look

good in marching band? He was a dweeb--all he needed were thick glasses and a pocket protector--but he didn't seem to care and soon neither did she. Paula listened to Conrad tell her about his marching band days in college and the group he played with now. He also told her about and his grandmother's blackberry patch and how he used to help her harvest the berries and how she'd make pies. By the time their food arrived Paula had to admit that Conrad was rather cute *and* she liked him. His life sounded so different from hers. He was a second generation American, his grandparents on his mother's side came from Grenada and from Jamaica on his father's side, by way of Ghana. His parents had met at the party of a mutual college friend and married soon after. They'd had two children, and provided them with a nice upper middle class upbringing. In contrast, Paula had become a U.S. citizen just four years ago. His family seemed as if it could fit in a Norman Rockwell painting. Her family definitely wouldn't, but she wasn't sure she was ready to share yet.

"Well, it seems I've done all the talking," he said. "Tell me about your family."

"There's not much to say," Paula hedged. He seemed so regular she didn't want to shock him.

"I doubt it. I told you about my grandmother and her berry patch."

Paula hesitated then said, "My mother was my father's second wife."

He nodded. "My father had two wives. His first one died."

"My father had three wives at the *same* time," she clarified.

"Oh."

"I was brought up in a polygamous household." And when it became too contentious, her mother took her and her four siblings to live in Canada and then to America where they'd thrived. Her father visited, but rarely."

"Oh. My great-grandfather, the one from Ghana, could only afford one wife. He wasn't wealthy. I don't think I could handle three women at once. One woman is enough for me."

Paula smiled, wanting to believe him. Most men wanted more than one woman. "How about a mistress?"

His mouth quirked in a quick grin. "Is that a trick question?"

"No."

Conrad thought for a moment then again shook his head. "No, one woman is all I need."

Probably because he was so awkward around them, Paula thought. If he were savvier he'd change his stance. If he had women coming at him, he'd want his share. But perhaps that's why he made a good catch. He wouldn't be the kind of man a woman needed to worry about. But then again he could be lying.

"How about you?"

Paula took a sip of her drink then carefully set it down. "Me?"

"Would you want more than one man?"

"No, one's enough for me."

"Are you sure?"

"Perfectly." She had a friend who was juggling two

guys who adored her. Instead of feeling envious, Paula felt stressed at the thought of trying to keep two men happy at the same time.

"I guess that's another thing we have in common."

"Yes."

Paula was relieved that Conrad didn't make her background seem like something strange or weird. When she'd first arrived, new friends and acquaintances treated her life like a curiosity. From what he shared, it was evident that his family was more established in Western ways than hers. He was the eldest of two and had grown up in Pennsylvania to a surgeon, his father and scientist, his mother. Paula on the other hand, had twelve brothers and sisters. The first wife had four children, the second wife, her mother, had five (she lost one in childbirth), the third wife had three. And she had scores of relatives, all envious of their American ties, always begging for sponsorship or money. Once she'd finished her university studies, she'd given what she could, but it never seemed enough. Soon the requests no longer came by airmail, but filled her e-mail on her computer, forcing her to close her account for awhile.

"You can only do what you can, Paula," her mother always told her. "Besides, your father is well established back home, and he and his brothers are all doing well. Live your life. Stop feeling guilty for your blessings." But she had felt guilty. Guilty that life for her was one without much struggle, and she cherished the freedom she had, as a woman, not having to face being married off as soon as she came of age. Although she struggled with that freedom, because her mother thought it was wrong.

Everyone expected her to marry and she hadn't succeeded yet. In truth, she hadn't had as much interest in it as she should.

Thankfully, she had come to terms with what she could and couldn't do for others, and over the years the requests had slowed to a trickle. Her status as an unmarried woman, however, continued to be a sore spot.

They chatted some more then she saw something in Conrad's jacket move. At first she was certain she was hallucinating. *"Why would anything be moving under his coat?"* she wondered, sure it had been the trick of the light. But then she saw it again.

"What's that?" she asked.

Conrad glanced down at his plate. "Vegetable roti. Want some?"

Paula shook her head. "No, not what are you eating, what's under your jacket?"

He blinked. "My jacket?"

"Yes." Paula leaned forward and lowered her voice. "I saw something move." She pointed and her voice cracked when she spoke. "It did it again!"

Conrad glanced down then swore. "I forgot I put her in there."

Paula widened her eyes. "Put what in where? Please don't tell me it's an animal."

He flashed a sheepish grin.

"A rat?"

"No, I wouldn't do that."

"Then what is it?"

"My kitten. I was going to drop her off at my brother's but then I saw the lady with the flat tire and helped her.

Then when I got back in the car Wispy, that's her name because she's just a wisp of a thing, was crying so I put her inside my coat pocket because that always calms her down then I completely forgot about her and drove straight here."

"Well, she's obviously woken up."

He gently patted the lump inside his jacket pocket. "Don't worry she'll go back to sleep."

"Are you serious?"

"Don't believe me? Don't worry she's harmless." He opened his coat pocket and a little gray head with large green eyes popped out and stared at her.

TWO

"Then what did you do?" Paula's Aunt Miriam asked the next day as the two ate from a large bag of kale chips while Paula helped her aunt organize her bookkeeping. Her aunt ran a small shop and Paula helped her keep it profitable. They sat in Paula's apartment and Paula always enjoyed spending time with her.

But as she reviewed the calculations, her mood dimmed. "She's still skimming money."

Her aunt shrugged. She knew her daughter wasn't trustworthy, but didn't care. "As long as it remains small who cares?"

"I do. I have to talk to her."

"Leave it. Now you haven't answered my question."

"About what?" Paula said absently, making more calculations.

Miriam snatched the calculator from her. "The kitten."

"Oh. He went back to eating as if nothing had happened."

"So, are you going to see him again?"

Paula stared at her aunt. She considered her a trusted confidant, but now wondered if she'd made a mistake. Her aunt was an attractive woman who'd been a stunner in her youth. She'd married twice--marriages which she called heaven and hell. Her first husband had died in a car accident. After she became a widow for the second time, in her late fifties, when her second husband died from prostate cancer, she decided against remarrying. She was one of Paula's strongest critics when it came to the men she went out with, so Paula was surprised by her aunt's question. She'd expected a tart dismissal of her blind date.

"Did you or did you not just hear a word I said? He's clumsy, he's strange. He plays the tuba for goodness sakes."

"Musicians are sexy."

"Not this one."

"But it sounded like you enjoyed yourself."

"I did," Paula admitted, surprised by how much she had. She sat back and smiled. "I mean, he has a great sense of humor and is really easy to talk to." She reached for the calculator; her aunt moved it out of reach. "But he's just not my type," she insisted, ready to change the subject. "I doubt I'm his type either. I don't expect him to call me." She held out her hand.

Her aunt handed her the calculator like a petulant child. "Pity, he sounded interesting."

"Weird."

Her aunt waved a kale chip at her. "He's better than Baloney."

"His name was Bennett."

Her aunt bit into the chip. "My name suits him better."

"You think everyone's better than Bennett."

"I was right."

"You were biased."

"He was no good, right? Admit it."

Paula made a face then munched on her snack. She remembered first describing Bennett to her aunt and all the excited feeling she'd felt then.

"Run fast," her aunt had said in a flat tone.

"I don't want to," Paula replied. "He's amazing. He's a chef and starting his own restaurant. There's already a buzz around him."

Aunt Miriam sniffed. "Like vultures circling something dead."

"He's funny, attractive--"

"Looks aren't everything."

"So everyone says, but they're wrong. It helps."

Aunt Miriam shook her head. "You'll get bored with him."

"No, he's exciting and driven."

But she'd been right. Paula had gotten bored and the restaurant closed within a year due to poor management. Bennett talked a good game but could never follow through. He bought a food truck, but then lost interest, later he opened a corner store, which was also a flop. He had what he deemed an "artistic temperament," which she soon discovered really meant swinging between pouting lows and raging tantrum highs. He'd sounded so perfect--charming, handsome, daring--but seemed to be more suited for a fairy-tale than a real life. In reality he was a bore. Their conversations never went beyond how talented and smart he was and how unfair the world was to him.

After Bennett she'd fallen for Edwin, a successful businessman by way of Cameroon. He was different. He wasn't a dreamer and was more down to earth. He was ambitious, handsome and cultured. Everything her mother expected her to look for in a man.

"Another bore," her aunt had told Paula after meeting him.

"What do you mean another bore?"

"I mean another pretty sounding man who will certainly not translate into a long happy relationship."

"He's attractive, successful--"

"All flash and no substance."

Paula rolled her eyes. "You've met him only once."

"That's all I needed. Actually, more than I needed. I know men. I married two, remember?"

"Yes, heaven and hell. When will you tell me exactly what that means?"

"Isn't it obvious?"

"I liked Uncle Jules."

"So did everyone else."

"I hardly remember Uncle Wale," Paula said, referring to her aunt's first husband. She remembered a quiet man who smelled like nutmeg and gave great hugs. Uncle Jules was funny and lively and wore expensive cologne.

"What was the difference? Why was Uncle Wale heaven and Uncle Jules hell?"

"You'll figure it out one day," Aunt Miriam said in a cryptic tone.

"Edwin loves me."

"Really? How do you know?"

"He tells me all the time."

Aunt Miriam shook her head. "If he has to keep telling you he doesn't mean it."

"I don't believe that. Some men are more verbal than others."

"You think you're lucky. But instead you should think he's lucky."

"You're playing with words."

"And you're not listening to me."

Paula didn't listen because she didn't want to. What her aunt was saying sounded silly. Why should she worry about a man being lucky to have her? Or, how many times he told her he loved her? She had been convinced that it was only because her aunt thought she was the moon and the stars that she thought men should feel the same way about her. But from her experience, Paula knew men didn't think that way.

At least Edwin hadn't. Her aunt had been right again. He was all flash and soon the shine wore thin. He never cared what she had to say or how her day had been. No matter how much she'd dressed up, it was never good enough for him.

Like a film stuck in a loop, his criticisms were always the same: "Are you going to wear that?" "Don't you have something better to wear?" "I don't like your hair that way." She'd stayed with him because her mother had been impressed, and she'd been flattered by how often people said they looked good together. But after nine months of dating, Paula discovered she wasn't the polished image he wanted to display. He quickly replaced her with his newly-hired personal assistant.

Which was why she'd accepted the blind date with Conrad; she'd stopped trusting herself. She'd never gone on blind dates before because she didn't trust other people to select the right person for her. People underestimated her. They saw an attractive woman with a lot of degrees and success and assumed she was either frigid or high maintenance. But that was far from the truth. She liked science fiction movies and rock climbing. She liked to go kayaking and party all night in clubs. But now that she was past thirty-five, suddenly her lifestyle was unacceptable. Friends worried for her because she'd never married and they were convinced that it was better to be divorced than never to have been married.

Her family felt the same way. Her two brothers and one sister were married, and her youngest sister was engaged. And she was only nineteen!

"Why is it better to marry and divorce?" she'd once asked her aunt.

"Because men will think there's something wrong with you if you've never been married."

"Why can't it be that I'm choosy?"

"It's the law of nature. We as humans only like what other people like, and society says a woman should be married, or at least have tried. So, even if it's a bad match just find someone or you'll end up alone."

And she didn't want that. Even though the thought of settling down with just anyone made her cringe. But it had been the catalyst to agree to Tamara's pestering about the blind date. At first she'd been irritated by her friend's selection. She'd expected better. Didn't her best friend know they weren't right for each other? But the more Paula thought about her meeting with Conrad, the more she began to reconsider. Their conversation had been smooth and, if she was honest, she knew she liked him. Unfortunately, there had been no spark. No passionate chemistry and he didn't have the look.

"No, he won't call me and I'm fine with that," Paula said, no longer sure if she believed it.

BUT SHE WAS WRONG. A week later Conrad called and asked her out to a comedy club, and to her surprise she heard herself quickly saying yes. This time there were no spilled glasses or secret kittens. Instead they spent the evening enjoying a playful banter with the comedian, who heckled Conrad about his large size and clothes. "I think I saw that jacket before on the original version of the *Incredible Hulk*." The crowd laughed and Conrad took no offense and Paula felt relaxed. He was confident and didn't take himself too seriously. He was comfortable in his skin. Yes, he could be awkward at times, but she found it more endearing than annoying. As they walked back to his car, she shivered at the chilly evening wishing she'd brought something warmer to wear. Conrad took off his coat and handed it to her. It was his gray tweed jacket and it still had the smudge near the hem. She'd rather freeze than be caught wearing it so she offered him a smile and said she was okay.

Although she rejected his offer, Paula found herself saying yes to trips to the museum, bicycle riding, movies, and outdoor concerts. But there were still differences between them that she had to address. Like his clothes. He wasn't a great dresser and if she wanted to introduce him to anyone he had to present himself well.

"I have a networking event coming up and I need a date," she told him one day after they'd had lunch. "But first I need to know if you have a suit."

"Of course I have a suit."

"I want to see it." Minutes later she stood in front of his closet and frowned. His kitten Wispy kept brushing up against her leg and purring. She glanced down at her, curious. "Why does she keep doing that?"

"Because she likes you. Give her a quick pat and she'll stop."

"Oh." Paula bent and awkwardly stroked the kitten. She'd never had pets and had never been interested but had to admit it was cute. However, she had come to his house for a reason. She straightened and looked at his clothes again. The suit was awful. She lifted a sleeve then released it as if it were crawling with ants. "Where did you get this?"

"It's tailor made. All my suits are because of my size."

She turned to him surprised. "Really?"

He nodded.

She lifted the suit to make sure. It looked off the rack but she could see some minor alterations had been made.

However it was not superior quality. "How much did you pay?" When he told her the amount she swore. He was being ripped off. His tailor had been gleefully stealing money from him for years. Conrad was too nice and trusting. She tossed the suit on the bed in disgust. "Do you still have the receipt?"

"Uh...yes."

"Get it."

"Why?"

"We're getting you a refund."

WHEN SHE MET MR. STEWART, the tailor, she expected a beady little man with clammy hands. He was nothing of the sort. Instead he had an engaging grin and warm, firm handshake. She wasn't fooled. She handed him the suit. "There's been an error. He wants the suit for which you charged him. Not this poor imitation. And yes, please argue with me on this. I'm in a bad mood and will enjoy making your life miserable. No, don't look at him, look at me. You charged him for cloth you didn't provide, a stitch you didn't do and I could go on, but I'll save that for my lawyer."

"Lawyer? There's no need for that. It's just a simple misunderstanding."

"Fix it."

Minutes later they left the shop with a promise of three new suits in the dimensions that Paula expected. Conrad held the car door open for her, amazed. "You're incredible."

"I know. When he calls to say they're ready, let me know. *I'll* pick them up."

Conrad got into the driver's side. "I'm sure he didn't mean any harm. He knows I have money."

"That's even worse. You should wear clothes according to your status."

Conrad laughed. "I don't care about that."

"It's bad business to treat customers the way he does. He doesn't respect you and you should always command respect. I don't ever want you going back there. I know a tailor you can trust."

He didn't go back but the final three suits he got from Mr. Stewart were stunning. After two months of seeing each other, Paula knew he wanted their relationship to become more serious--she wasn't sure yet, especially when there were still other options. And one day one of those options showed up.

THREE

"Paula?"

Paula turned towards the voice. She'd been waiting for Conrad to meet her. She was attending a key networking event to gain more clients for her company. It had been her aunt's idea. "If he cares about you, he'll show up. It's important for a man to show interest in your career." And he had. He'd just left to get them both drinks and she was alone, ready to mingle. The man who'd spoken her name was beautiful and so sinfully hot he could have made the sun sweat. "Yes?"

"I thought so. I was in your class at the University of Maryland." Paula had been an adjunct professor at the university for two years, teaching business finance and commerce.

Yes, she remembered him. Andre Bell. He'd set the campus on fire, not just for his athletic ability, taking the university to a national basketball championship, but he was smart, and was admired by all.

"How are you?" he asked.

Paula fought to get her mouth in working order. "Well."

"You look great. If you're done with all your meet and greet, I'd like to take you out for coffee."

He could take her out for coffee, tea, soda whatever he wanted. She really wanted to go. This was her chance. She could leave right now; send a text to Conrad and say that something had come up. He'd understand. It was tempting, but something made her stop. "Sorry, I can't. I'm here with someone."

"Someone special?"

"No, we're just friends," she said, wanting to leave the door open for a second invite.

"Maybe another time then."

Yes. She glanced up and saw Conrad carrying a plate of desserts. He looked great in his new suit. Not debonair, but presentable. He was just a few feet away when he tripped and a strawberry tart landed on the front of his shirt leaving a bright pink stain. Paula briefly hung her head. *Figures.* She glanced at Andre and saw his mouth quirk as he tried not to laugh.

"Sorry I took so long," Conrad said handing her the plate. "I got chatting with this guy about his business that really needs to be restructured. I got his card for you and gave him your name. I told him you were one of the best." He fumbled for the card he had placed in his pocket. "Ah, yes here it is."

"Thanks," Paula first glanced at the card then stared when she read the name.

Andre glanced over her shoulder and read the name then gave a low whistle.

Paula stared at Conrad amazed. "How did you get this?"

Conrad frowned. "I just told you."

"Do you know who this is?" She didn't let him answer. "He's a known entrepreneur. He turns businesses into multimillion dollar empires. I'm a nobody."

"No you're not. He said he could use your services."

"He was probably just being nice," Andre said.

Conrad shot him a glance and stretched out his hand. It appeared like a warm friendly gesture, but there was a chill to his tone. "And you are?"

"Andre Bell."

"This is a former student of mine," Paula said.

Conrad nodded. "I see. Well, you may not have much confidence in Paula, but I do. He wasn't being nice."

Andre grinned. "I didn't mean to offend you it's just that guys like that usually come to these events to throw their money around, get their names known, then leave. They don't need help."

"He does."

Paula lightly touched Conrad's arm not wanting him to argue. Andre was probably right but Conrad had such a good heart he probably wouldn't know the difference.

The two men couldn't be more different. It was almost painfully stark--one looked like a champion golden retriever, the other a loyal bloodhound.

"I'd better go," Andre said. "Talk to you later, Paula. Nice to meet you Conrad."

Conrad nodded and Paula merely waved.

"Old friend?" Conrad asked, watching Andre get up and walk over to another guest.

"I told you, I met him at the university."

Conrad was quiet a moment then looked at her. "Did he ask you out?"

"What?"

He shrugged. "I wouldn't blame him."

Paula stood feeling restless and guilty, although she had no reason to. "Let's go. You need to change your shirt."

He gently tugged her back down. "Relax. It won't stain."

"You've done this before?"

"You're avoiding my question."

Paula picked up a ladyfinger then softly said, "Yes, he asked me to have coffee."

"And what did you say?"

"Guess."

He briefly closed his eyes. "You said 'No, my boyfriend wouldn't like it.'"

Boyfriend? Funny she'd never even thought of that. Had they really gotten to that stage? Did she want to?

Conrad sighed and looked at her. "So that's not what you said?"

"I did say no," she said wondering why the feeling of guilt continued to linger. They'd never talked about being exclusive.

"But you didn't say I was your boyfriend."

"I didn't know you were."

"What do you think I am?"

"Just a friend."

Conrad shook his head and offered her one of his rare crooked smiles. "I like you too much to be just a friend. If you don't want more, then let's stop this now."

"No, I just..."

"Go out with him. If he's the one you want to be with, just let me know."

"Conrad don't," Paula said now feeling anxious. She playfully nudged him with her elbow. "Come on. You know I like you."

"Go out with him then we'll both know how much."

"YOU'RE GIVING UP A GOOD GUY," Aunt Miriam said as Paula prepared for her date with Andre. She'd asked to borrow her aunt's gold necklace and her aunt had insisted on coming over with it.

"I'm not giving him up. I'm just taking a break."

"And in the meantime someone else will snap him up."

"No one has so far."

"That's because women are stupid."

Paula turned to her aunt surprised. "I thought you were a feminist."

"I am, but that doesn't stop me from seeing the failings of our sex. If we're not indulging in unhealthy diets or falling for beauty fads we're choosing the wrong men."

"It's just coffee."

"For now," Aunt Miriam said with a knowing look.

HER DATE that evening was almost magical. Everything was perfect. Unlike Conrad, Andre arrived on time beautifully dressed carrying a single white rose. There were no awkward silences. The conversation was fascinating. Unlike Bennett, Andre was established, so he wasn't one of those high flying dreamers she used to attract; and, unlike Edwin, he listened to her. He was warm, funny and gracious. And she knew they looked wonderful together.

"This was great. Let's make it dinner next time," he said. He walked beside her as they navigated an uneven pavement outside the restaurant.

A second date? Really? Before she could reply a metal construction sign dropped from its hold and struck her arm, tearing her sleeve and cutting her arm and hand.

"Are you okay?" Andre asked.

"Yes, I'm fine," Paula said a little stunned.

He looked at the cut and grimaced. "Oh that looks nasty. When you get home you'd better put some ice on that."

"I will," she said, awkwardly adjusting her torn sleeve and moving her hand out of view. "Thanks for a great time."

He kissed her on the cheek then whispered, "Think about dinner."

"Yes." Paula walked to her car, his warm breath still tingling her ear and the scent of his cologne lingering. She got inside her car, slammed the car door shut then swore. Now that she was alone she didn't have to pretend that her arm and hand didn't hurt like hell. Fortunately, her car was an automatic, not a stick shift. Once at home,

Paula took off her torn blouse and cleaned her cuts with some hydrogen peroxide, put a bandage on both, then grabbed a drink from her fridge and noticed Conrad's birthday circled on her calendar. Treating a friend for his birthday wasn't wrong. She'd gotten him tickets to a 3D feature at a small obscure theatre she knew he liked. She decided to call him. It had only been a week, yet she'd started to miss his voice. "Do you have any plans for Saturday?" she asked once he'd picked up.

"I'll be in Maui with my model girlfriend."

She chuckled. "Before you go I have a treat for you."

"Okay."

IT HAD BEEN a couple weeks since she had been with him at the networking party, and a lot had happened. The contact Conrad had given her from the networking event had come through; he had signed a lucrative contract with her company and she had been nominated for an award recognizing young business professionals. They were two things she was surprisingly eager to tell him about. That evening, Paula took her time getting dressed. She wasn't sure why, then just figured it was because it was his birthday and she wanted it to be special. When he opened the door she waved the tickets and smiled. "Happy Birthday."

He frowned. "What happened to your hand?"

Paula glanced down. She'd forgotten about her injury. "I was attacked by a road sign," she said with a laugh. "The wind knocked it over and it tore my blouse cutting my arm and hand. Are you sure you didn't organize it?" she asked trying to lighten his intense expression.

"Me?"

"Yes, I was out with Andre and I know you didn't want me to be." She'd meant it as a joke, but Conrad didn't smile.

"Did he take you to the hospital to get checked?"

"I didn't need to get checked. It was just a cut."

"By a large metal object. Did he apply antiseptic?"

"He didn't do anything."

"Except drive you home?"

"Why would he drive me home when we both came in separate cars?"

"Has he called you?"

"For another date?" she asked surprised by the change in topic. Conrad looked angry, she'd never seen him like this. "No, not yet."

His jaw twitched. "I meant did he call to see if you were okay."

"You're getting upset. Come on, let's go."

"I'm not upset."

"Yes you are, you're clenching your jaw." She playfully patted his cheek. "Forget about it."

He pulled her inside and led her into his living room. "Sit down."

"We'll be late."

He shot her a glance and she sat. He ran down the hall.

"Stop!"

He turned to her startled.

"You're wearing flip flops."

"So?"

"You shouldn't run in flip flops. You could slip out of them and break your leg or something, especially going down the stairs. This is not an emergency."

"I haven't broken anything so far so you can relax." He disappeared into the bathroom. Wispy jumped up on the couch. Paula stroked her and the kitten began to purr. "Your Daddy is in a funny mood."

"No, he's annoyed." Conrad came back into the living room carrying a First Aid kit. He sat. "Show me your arm first."

"We're going to be late."

"Then move faster."

Paula showed him her arm. He cleaned it with some antiseptic. She winced, it was still very sore.

"I'm sorry," he said then put on a new bandage. He cleaned the top of her hand then bit his lip and raised his eyes to hers. "Did he ask you out again?"

Paula met his gaze. It was so serious and sincere she couldn't help smiling. "Has anyone ever told you that you have nice eyes?"

He sighed. "Don't play with me, Paula."

"I'm not. I really like your eyes. Even when they're serious as they are now." She waved the tickets. "And you're going to miss your birthday gift."

"Did you say yes?"

"To a second date?"

He nodded.

"I didn't say anything. That's when the sign attacked me."

"I see."

"I told you to forget about it."

"Make me."

"Is that a challenge?"

He nodded.

She brushed her mouth against his. "Now let's go." She stood.

Conrad stood too and pulled her close. "Not yet." His lips met hers and his kiss reminded her of him. It was like hot cinnamon chocolate. Warm and sweet. A habit she could definitely get used to. He drew away and searched her face, but she could tell he didn't find what he was looking for because his eyes had a guarded look she didn't like. For some reason she didn't like being the source of his disappointment or unhappiness. She liked him a lot, although most times she wasn't quite sure why. Paula stood on her tip toes and again brushed her lips against his, wishing she could make his guarded look disappear. Although it was a light quick touch, her lips tingled, but his wary look remained. At times she felt there was a chasm between them she couldn't cross, but she didn't want to think of that. She grabbed his coat. "Now, let's go."

THE MOVIE WAS a bomb but they laughed throughout at how awful it was. Afterwards, since it was still warm outside, they walked along the Potomac while she shared her news about her new client and the award nomination. Then Conrad treated her to dinner at a fancy restaurant in the heart of downtown, even though it was his birthday.

"I know the owner," he said. "I helped him get started. So order whatever you want."

She did with eagerness. That feeling left her once they waited twenty minutes just for the stale bread that finally arrived at their table. The main meal was not much better. She took one bite, set her fork down and folded her arms. "Get the chef," she told the waitress.

"Is there a problem?" the young woman asked with a tentative smile.

Paula gritted her teeth. "Yes."

The waitress left and Conrad leaned towards her. "What's wrong?"

"Don't take a single bite."

"But--"

The chef, Judson Delord, arrived at the table. A hearty looking young man with silvery blonde hair and a tan that seemed to come by way of a cheap tanning booth rather than the sun. He gave Conrad a warm greeting. "What can I do for you two?"

"Give us what we ordered," Paula said.

"What?"

"We ordered the seafood platter. Unfortunately, what I see on my plate is rice that is only partially cooked, and scallops that had clearly been frozen on their way here rather than fresh. I won't even ask what this pile of mush is supposed to be, crab cakes perhaps."

"All our food is fresh."

She raised her plate. "Since you don't believe me, have a taste."

Judson hesitated then lowered his voice. "Look fresh is expensive. Most people can't tell the difference."

Conrad set his napkin on the table. "Funny, that doesn't sound like an apology."

Judson glanced at his friend then sighed. "I'm sorry."

Paula pointed at Conrad. "He knows the owner."

"Paula--" Conrad said.

She ignored him. "Give me a reason not to call the owner."

"I'm the owner," Judson said.

"What?"

"That's what I was trying to say," Conrad said.

"Is this how you treat your friends? Cutting costs at the expense of your business's success?"

Judson stiffened. "I'm making money."

"You could make more."

His eyes lit up. "How?"

"I charge for information like that." She stood. "Let's go." She left the restaurant before Conrad could stop her.

He caught up with her a block away. "Where are you going?"

"Home."

"You know I'll take you home."

"I'm so angry."

"He said he'd cook us something else for free."

Paula stopped and stared up at him. "I wouldn't even nibble bread he buttered. How dare he smile at you while feeding you garbage at the same time? You said you helped him finance this?"

Conrad took her arm and moved off the sidewalk to

stand under the awning of a building. "Yes, he said he didn't know."

"Of course he knew. He's the chef *and* the owner. He's just sloppy."

"He's willing to learn."

"You're lying. I bet he hates my guts."

"Doesn't matter. You were right. He wants to hear your ideas and he's willing to pay you."

She frowned. "I doubt he can afford it."

"I can."

"Will you profit too?"

"Yes."

She glanced back in the direction of the restaurant then looked at him."Then I'll do it for you."

He gave her a brief hug. "Thank you."

"I'm still annoyed," she said but his warm embrace had improved her mood.

"I'm sorry. I hate to see you this upset."

"Don't apologize. It's not your fault." She paused. "Okay, maybe it's partly your fault. You're too under-standing. You have to command respect. Demand it. Don't you care what people think about you?"

"Not really."

"That's the problem. How people see you is the key to your power. It's the basis of every decision they'll make about you. You're the size of a redwood yet people treat you like a toothpick."

"The only opinions that matter to me are the ones from the people I care about."

Paula sighed. He was clueless and that frustrated her. But she'd fallen for a dreamer before so she couldn't blame him for being fooled. But as man he should know how important power was.

He grinned. "You can be quite fierce."

"I know."

He took her hand. "You mean a lot to me."

She smiled her bad mood disappearing. "I know that too."

They walked back to his car. "Have you ever gone berry picking?" he asked.

"No."

"Would you like to try?"

Berry picking. It was something new. "Sure, that sound interesting, but why berry picking?"

"It's the right time and my grandmother wants to meet you."

"Oh." Paula didn't mention that she hadn't thought of introducing him to any of her family. Perhaps one day soon. "I haven't said I'll be your girlfriend yet."

"I know. She still wants to meet you."

FOUR

THE FOLLOWING SATURDAY, Conrad took Paula on a comfortable, quiet drive, thirty minutes out of town. She didn't tell him that Andre had called her twice, and that she'd gone out for coffee with him. And Conrad didn't ask. Paula wondered why they got on so well, when there seemed to be so many differences between them. She liked to get to the point. He handled things in a laid back way. She still remembered seeing her first sight of snow at the age of eight, when they had arrived in Ontario, Canada in the middle of winter. He'd been skiing since he was four. His grandmother had a berry patch. Her grandmother lived a life of privilege and wouldn't know what manual labor was. Any chore she needed done, she would give to her housekeeper. Paula inwardly laughed thinking of how she'd guarded herself from telling her aunt and mother where he was taking her.

"Just to his grandmother's place, she has a berry

patch." she'd told the two women at lunch. Her mother liked to invite her over monthly to have lunch with her at her apartment. Calls from her mother always felt more like summons than invitations. About every two weeks her mother had a new outfit made. She pretended to want her daughter and sister over for their opinions and to eat, but in truth she wanted compliments. Which they always gave. Today the menu included baked plantain, steamed greens and curried goat. Her mother wore an expensive lace gown, which she planned to wear to an upcoming wedding.

"Why?" her mother asked. Her mother looked just like Paula, except she was taller, and wore glasses. She had striking features but was not as beautiful as her sister Miriam. She still turned heads and always looked as if she were ready for a portrait.

"He wants me to see it."

"How much does he make?"

"Six figures."

"Low, middle, or high?"

Her sister sent her a look. "Does it matter? Six figures is enough."

"More is always better than enough."

"I don't know," Paula said.

"Find out. You should know information like that by now."

"What's so special about a bloody berry patch?" Aunt Miriam asked.

"Watch your language," her sister said.

Aunt Miriam only rolled her eyes then looked at her niece. "Tell us the truth."

"I am," Paula said. "We're going berry picking."

"What? Is that an American slang for something?"

"No, we are actually going to pick berries."

Her mother scowled. "Doesn't the woman have workers to do that? What's the point of having property if you have to toil the land yourself?" Her mother was averse to manual work of any kind, including preparing a cup of tea.

Paula smiled. "I think it will be fun."

"Be careful," her mother warned pointing at her. "He may just want to see how hard you'll work. You want a man who will take care of you not vice versa. They can be sly in their ways. "

"Mother, it is simply a trip to his grandmother's berry patch nothing more."

Her mother frowned, but for some reason her aunt began to grin.

Paula wondered about that smile as Conrad drove up to a lovely colonial house nestled among what looked like woods. The house was impeccably kept, with a lovely garden in the front, displaying a wide variety of blooming flowers and off to the side, Paula caught a glimpse of a neatly tended garden bursting with an array of vegetables. They walked up a paved walkway and then Conrad knocked on the front door. A tall woman, with sharp eagle-like eyes, answered and hugged Conrad then grinned at Paula.

She extended her hand. "You must be Charlotte."

Paula paused. "No."

"Juanita?"

"No."

"Giselle?"

Paula shook her head.

"Stop teasing her Gran," Conrad said in good humor. "You know she's the only woman I've ever brought here. Come on."

His grandmother giggled like a naughty school girl and then took her hand. "Oh, that was lots of fun. You should have seen your face."

"Well, I wouldn't blame him if he'd brought all of his girlfriends here." Paula said. "This place is beautiful."

"Flattery will get you everything. Now let's go pick some berries." His grandmother moved quickly, with a speed that belied her age of eighty-one. She led them to the back of the house where several large cane blackberry bushes grew. She handed Paula and Conrad a basket each.

Within seconds Paula realized she didn't know what she was doing. Conrad and his grandmother seemed to have a rhythm she couldn't pick up, but she didn't care. She was enjoying herself and imagined the sweet blackberry pie they would bake later.

His grandmother came up to Paula and looked into her basket. "You're doing it all wrong."

"Wrong?"

"Yes. The way you're choosing the berries. The ones that are hard and shiny are usually bitter inside. Instead, you want to look for the ones like this." His grandmother reached out and pulled several berries from deep inside the bush. "You want to look for berries that are sort of dull, plump, and undamaged, rich with color that almost fall away in your hand."

"Oh."

His grandmother looked down at the ugly looking berry. "Not attractive I know, but they're delicious." She popped several in her mouth. "The best way to find the berry you like is to taste them."

"You're the expert."

"Yes I am." She sent Paula a sidelong glance then lowered her voice. "You pick your men that way too, don't you? Don't look so shocked. You wouldn't be the first. Most women do. They go for what they see on the outside or for what *sounds* good and not what *is* good." She looked over at Conrad who was busy eating a handful of berries. "I know he doesn't look like much, but he's a solid man. Most women pass him up because he doesn't meet the typical standard of charm or attractiveness."

"He's a nice man." Paula continued picking, uneasy with how accurate his grandmother was.

"He's more than that but you don't see it. He's 'black gold', just like the finest blackberries. So do us both a favor and break up with him before you break his heart."

Paula looked at her surprised. "What?"

"I know your type. I like you. I really do, but not for my grandson. He needs someone who really sees how special he is and that woman isn't you."

"Mrs.--"

"I can tell that you're the kind of woman who likes to get to the point and so do I. I don't suffer fools gladly. I love my grandson and when he finds the right woman I'll know it." She tapped her chest. "Just like I know how to pick berries, I know how to read people. That man you have hanging on the side." She began to grin. "Thought I didn't know about him? Yes, I do. Conrad told me you still want to be free. You want your options open. Well, I'm here to tell you that option number two is perfect for you. You want a suave, sophisticated man who looks good in a dinner jacket and charms clients, so go after him. He's who you deserve. Leave my grandson alone." She narrowed her eyes and hardened her tone. "And if you stay with Conrad to spite me, I promise I'll make you pay." She turned and left.

Paula stared at the older woman's back, speechless. Sugar and spice she was not. She didn't think she was good enough for Conrad? Maybe she didn't think *any* woman would be. Who did she think she was to tell her about the man she deserved? She was a catch and no one would tell her what to do.

She walked over to Conrad and looped her arm through his. She glanced up and saw his grandmother tighten her lips. Paula didn't care. She glanced down and looked into his basket and saw it was full. "You're really good at this."

"I've had the practice."

"Your Gran let me know I was doing it all wrong so I had to start over."

"Better to start over than have a basket filled with bitter fruit."

"That almost sounds like a proverb."

"I'm a man of hidden talents. Have you tasted one yet?"

"I thought I'd wait for the pie."

"No, nothing's better than a ripe fruit."

"Said Eve to Adam."

"This is not that kind of garden." He held a berry out to her.

She could have taken the berry from him. She could have fed herself, but she didn't. Paula opened her mouth and let him place the berry inside.

He was right. There was nothing like the fresh juicy taste of a ripe, juicy, blackberry and having someone you were quickly growing fond of feeding it you.

"Well?"

"It's delicious. Help me pick some more."

"WHAT WAS IT LIKE?" her Aunt Miriam asked the next day when she and Paula's mother came to visit. She knew there was no way of stopping them.

"It was wonderful," Paula said setting tea on the table. "We picked berries and laughed and then his grandmother made this delicious pie. She gave me one to take home."

"How is he with her?"

"They're very close."

"That's a bad sign," her mother said.

"Why?"

"He might always compare you to her."

"I doubt he expects me to turn into a pie making, berry picking woman."

"You never know."

Aunt Miriam shook her head. "Don't listen to your mother. She married flash and I married substance. Substance lasts longer."

"How would you know with two dead husbands?" her sister chided.

"Only one man lasts longer in my heart. Had he lived it would have been heaven."

Paula's mother shook her head. "So called 'substance' can only last you so long. It was your father's connections that got us here. He treated me well...I just didn't like the household. But I was well taken care of." Her mother tried to sound offended, but they knew she wasn't. Paula was well aware of her father's contributions. Neither she nor her siblings had lacked for anything when her mother had up and left her father. He was out of the country at the time, and she had just gotten into one of her many fights with his third wife. She was the most recent addition to their household, and had taken an instant dislike to Paula's mother and her children. She was always complaining and shouting at them, but one day she went too far and struck Paula with a wooden kitchen spoon, leaving a large welt on the back of her arm. Her mother had never raised her hand to any of her children, and without her husband being there for protection, decided she didn't want her children to grow up in a home with quarreling and, worst of all, violence.

Her mother had called her father and within four days they were on a plane, with several suitcases carrying all their belongings, heading for Toronto, Canada, where a friend of her father was waiting for them. He had been very helpful, securing a house for them, enrolling them in school and introducing them to the African immigrant community there. At first, her mother regretted her decision, there were no housemaids, or drivers to run her errands, but Paula and her siblings all pitched in to help. Once they all finished middle school, her mother decided to move to Maryland, where her Aunt Miriam lived. Her mother still lived on the monthly stipend her father sent for them. Paula had never been able to understand why they stayed married, but over the years she had accepted their relationship for what it was.

Unlike her father, Conrad wasn't wealthy. He wasn't handsome. He wasn't charming. Just solid. Nothing to brag about. Could she handle that? How would she be around her friends whose husbands were far more dashing? She had one friend whose husband wasn't attractive but at least he was wealthy and showered her friend with gifts and affection. Then there was another friend whose husband was not wealthy but was drool-worthy gorgeous. When he walked into a room, all heads turned. Then there was Tamara, who had gotten both a wealthy and attractive catch and was the envy of their close-knit Afro-Caribbean community. But Tamara hadn't worried about Conrad being neither wealthy nor handsome, she'd liked him and had thought he would be a good catch for her. She didn't need his money, she had plenty of her own and he wasn't intimated by her income, although some men had been. Yet she knew he wouldn't pass her mother's scrutiny and she still had doubts.

"Choose a man who won't shame you," her mother said.

Paula listened knowing that Conrad wouldn't stand a chance.

HER MOTHER'S words came back to Paula a couple of weeks later when she received the award announcement. She'd won. Paula stared at the announcement stunned. All her work and sacrifice on her job had been worth it. First she'd seen her company's business nearly triple after signing the contract with the entrepreneur; and now she'd won a prestigious award. She had to tell Conrad. She reached for the phone, but before she picked it up, it rang. She glanced at the number. It was Andre. She hesitated then answered.

"Congratulations," he said.

"You heard already?"

"I knew when the announcements would come out and checked."

"I can't believe it."

"You worked hard. You'll love the banquet."

She paused. "Banquet?"

"Yes, that's when you'll receive your prize."

How could she have forgotten about the banquet? That's when all her peers would be there. She could imagine Conrad spilling his drink on a guest or staining his shirt again, the thought made her groan.

"Is something wrong?" Andre asked.

Yes. "No."

"You know, you haven't given me an answer about dinner."

Of course, Andre would never make a mistake like that. He moved easily through a crowd and people liked him. He'd make a great escort. That's all he would be. Conrad didn't need to know about the banquet and she'd tell him about the prize later.

"I've got something better in mind," she said.

FIVE

"I'm so proud of you!" her Aunt Miriam said giving her a fierce hug. Paula had stopped by her aunt's shop to tell her the good news. "What has Conrad said?"

"I haven't told him yet."

She narrowed her eyes. "Why not?"

"I'll tell him later."

"What are you hiding?"

"I've decided to go to the banquet with Andre."

"Why?"

"It will be better."

"For whom?" her aunt challenged.

"Both of us."

"I haven't even met him yet and you're already throwing him away?"

"I'm not thr--"

"Then why won't you take him?" she cut in.

"He's socially awkward. It's not the kind of

atmosphere where anything can go wrong. This night means a lot to me."

"You sound like your mother."

"She has a point. What he doesn't know--"

"Will hurt both of you."

"Don't be so dramatic."

"I don't care if he wears clown shoes, if you love him, you'll tell him. He has the right to know." She held her arms and shook her. "Listen to me on this: Tell Conrad."

But she didn't. Paula convinced herself it was best for both of them. After the banquet she would tell him how long and boring it was. How she wanted to save him the agony of having to dress up like a penguin in a tuxedo, which she knew he hated, and then they'd laugh about it. It would be fine, although it was hard not to tell him about the award. He'd been so supportive, but she only had to keep it from him for a little while. She could do that.

THE NIGHT of the banquet was perfection. Paula felt like a queen and reveled in the envious glances and whispered remarks from the women wondering who her date was and commenting on what a handsome pair they made. "See Dad, I'm a success," she thought as she left the stage holding her award. She hadn't realized that after so many years, his opinion still mattered, but now she was past it. Growing up she had wanted her father to be there to see her successes, but he never came. Over time, she and her siblings saw him only on a few occasions, and knew of him only as their "financial" provider and father in name only. Tonight she was beautiful, and successful, with a man at her side who projected the right image. She glanced at her aunt who was frowning and her mother who was beaming. She exited the ballroom and headed for the ladies' room.

"I can't believe you came with that smiley faced boy," her aunt said as she entered the room.

Paula touched up her lipstick then put the tube away. "Andre's really a great guy."

"I was hoping to meet Conrad tonight. I dressed up with extra care for him."

"You'll meet him another time," Paula said then turned and left, with her aunt following close behind.

Unfortunately, she was wrong. The moment she and her aunt left the ladies room, Conrad came out of another room. He saw her and smiled and walked towards her. He was dressed in a pair of casual jeans and a fitted polo jumper, carrying his tuba in a large case.

Paula halted, her heart hitting the floor. "Oh no."

"What?"

"That's him," Paula said in near panic, wishing she could hide.

"Who?"

Paula didn't get a chance to reply. Conrad stopped in front of them and grinned. "Wow. You look sensational." His gaze skimming over her dress with male admiration. "I'm here with my band, we just finished playing a gig for a retirement party. What's the occasion for you?"

"Um..." Paula turned to her aunt, hoping to change the topic. "This is my Aunt--"

"Miriam," he finished. He shook her hand. "A pleasure to finally meet you," he said his warm gaze making her blush.

"Thank you."

"There you are," Andre said coming up behind her. "You can't win an award and then disappear. People want to talk to you."

Paula glanced at Conrad. She didn't want to, but she had to see how the news affected him.

He didn't look surprised or hurt--he looked devastated. He was as clumsy at hiding his feelings as he was with his limbs, letting his heart spill out for everyone to see instead of keeping it guarded like a mature adult. It angered her. She wanted to shout at him *"No, you're doing it all wrong. You're supposed to act as if you don't care. As if I don't matter to you."* She hated how vulnerable he looked, how his emotions were so raw and real. But worse, she hated him making her feel vulnerable, because she was the cause. Had he kept his expression neutral she could have convinced herself that it was no big deal, but he'd not given her the option. She'd made a terrible mistake and would have to face the consequences.

"You won the award?" he said.

"She didn't tell you?" Andre said. "You're looking at the recipient of --"

"It's no big deal," Paula interrupted.

"Of course it's a big deal," Conrad said the pain in his eyes reflected in his voice. "Congratulations."

She couldn't say "thank you." She couldn't say anything. She just wanted to run. But there was no need.

Conrad turned and left and at that moment she knew she'd lost him. But she didn't want to. She raced after him and grabbed his sleeve. "I'm sorry."

"For what?" he said sounding defeated.

"I should have told you about the award and the banquet, but I know how much you hate crowds and--"

He spun around, his eyes hard and dark. "You think I wouldn't want to be by your side while you accept a prize you worked hard for? You should know me better than that. You know that no matter how much I hate dressing up, sit-down dinners and podium speeches, I would have come. I would have done anything for you. Now tell me the truth."

She took a step back unnerved by the ferocity of his tone. "The truth?"

"Yes. The truth is you didn't want me to come."

She wanted to lie but knew that he'd see right through her, just as he had the first time they'd met. "It was a stupid choice and a vain decision. I regretted it the moment I made it."

"But you didn't change your mind." He sighed with exasperation. "You know you matter to me, but the truth is *that* doesn't matter to you. I don't matter. I see that now."

"You've got it all wrong."

"Really? I am a man and I have an ego and desires just like any other man. And I can tell when the woman I care about is ashamed of me."

Paula shook her head and kept her voice steady. "I'm not ashamed."

He set his case down and folded his arms. "When

were you going to introduce me to your family? How about your friends? I've only met Tamara and that wasn't through you. When was I going to move past just being a friend? Did you think I'd be fine just holding your hand and giving you light kisses?" He lifted his tuba case. "I know I'm not perfect and I know I'm the right man for you, but I'm not going to wait around until you figure it out."

"Paula, time to go," Andre said, coming up behind her and gently pulling on her arm.

She didn't move. She felt like she was being torn in two directions.

Conrad glanced past her and looked at Andre then returned his gaze to her. "You do look good together."

She blinked back tears. "No, it's not like that. I--"

"Bye, Paula." He stared at her for a long moment then shook his head and walked away.

<hr>

THAT NIGHT PAULA lay in bed, praying for sleep that refused to come.

She felt like a butterfly whose wings had been ripped. She should forget him but she couldn't. She should bask in the approval of her mother and the envy of her friends, but she couldn't. She'd hurt him, but the most awful part was realizing that her selfish behavior showed how much she didn't deserve him. She deserved the dreamers and egos. They reflected a side of her she'd never taken the time to see. Not only had she picked berries that were shiny on the outside and bitter on the inside, she was one of them. Outwardly beautiful but inwardly sour.

She suddenly felt disgusted with herself. What had Conrad seen? How could he have cared for her? He was too kind, too giving, he deserved a woman who was the same. But that didn't stop her from wanting him. "Because I'm a selfish cow," she said aloud. His grandmother had been right not to trust her. She didn't deserve him. And she now understood what her aunt meant about her marriages: heaven and hell. It wasn't about the men but how the men made her feel. Not how the world viewed them but what others couldn't see, just as heaven and hell were whatever people imagined them to be.

But suddenly that didn't matter anymore, because she realized that too much was based on what was seen. Her mother had been the envy of her town for marrying the wealthy bank executive, Mr. Nelson Oyelowo and joining his household, but behind closed doors she had to endure the jealousies, unhappiness, and loneliness. Her mother had hated the loneliness the most. She never knew when her father would select her for the night and sleep in her bed. She hated how his last wife flaunted her beauty and schemed and manipulated him, and how blind he had become to the needs of his other wives.

As it was for blackberries, it really didn't matter what things looked like on the outside. What mattered was how things were on the inside. How they tasted. Paula remembered how the berry had melted in her mouth. She knew when people looked at Conrad they would see a large, shy man with an awkward gait. His former tailor had seen a soft hearted man he could sucker, his chef friend saw someone he could con. What she remembered of him was how beautiful and intelligent his eyes were; how he'd been the first person she'd called when she'd had to evacuate her apartment building in the middle of the night, due to a gas leak scare and how he'd stayed on the phone with her the entire time, his soothing voice making her feel cherished. How he'd highlighted all the best places for her to go to in the area for the best hiking trails or kayaking, even though he preferred a simple walk in the park or renting a tandem bicycle and going nowhere special. Most people wouldn't see his unselfish ways by just looking at him.

Paula suddenly realized those were the moments that truly counted. How he made her feel, not how everyone thought he looked or how they felt about him.

"SO WHAT ARE you going to do?" her aunt asked the next day, as Paula sat in her kitchen snacking on some dried fruit.

"There's nothing to do," she said feeling tired. "I can't get him back."

"You can at least try."

"You saw his face. It's hopeless."

"Yes, I saw his face and I know he loves you. You're making it hopeless by not even trying."

He may have loved her once, but not anymore. "He won't want me back."

"Is that fear talking?"

"Yes," Paula said fighting against tears. "I don't want to fail."

"Is he worth failing for?"

"It's me. I know he deserves better."

"Then be better."

"How?"

"You'll figure it out."

No, she wouldn't. She knew that no words, no gifts, no apologizes could heal the rift that had come between them. She wanted him to be happy. Isn't that what someone who loved did? They let that person go? If she wanted to prove how unselfish she was then that's what she would do. Or, she could become better. And she knew the person who could help her, although it would be a painful lesson.

PAULA STOOD on the porch of Conrad's grandmother's house for five minutes debating whether she should knock or leave. She hadn't called and wasn't expected, so she could just turn around and go. But that would be the coward's way and she wasn't going to be that...not anymore at least. She took a deep breath then knocked.

His grandmother opened the door. "I wondered when you'd make up your mind. What do you want?"

"I need to talk to you," Paula said.

"About what?" His grandmother said with a sniff. "I knew you'd break his heart."

"I want to heal it."

"I can't help you." She started to close the door.

Paula stopped her. "I deserve your anger and anything you want to throw at me, but I'm not leaving until I get to talk to you."

"Suit yourself." She shoved Paula back then slammed the door.

Paula glared at the door. The woman was stubborn but so was she. She sat on the porch and waited. His grandmother came out two hours later, startled to see Paula still there. She said nothing, turned, got in her car and drove away. Another two hours passed and she returned. She walked past Paula and went into her house. As the sun set, Paula considered sleeping in her car but didn't move. She was hungry but didn't care. She woke up later with a blanket covering her and the smell of coffee. She stretched her arms then blinked at the man sitting in front of her.

"Conrad?"

"My grandmother called me to get some intruder off of her property."

"I guess that would be me."

He stood avoiding her glance. "I put coffee in a thermos for your trip back."

"I gave it back."

He looked at her. "What?"

"The award. I gave it back. I didn't deserve it."

"Yes, you did. You worked hard for it."

"But life isn't just about actions and what people can see. It's about what's on the inside. The award should go to someone who's good both inside and out." She leaned forward and took a sip of the warm cup of coffee he held out to her, swallowed then fell on her knees in front of him in complete humility. "Please forgive me."

"Paula get up."

"Not until you forgive me."

Conrad pulled her to her feet. "Don't do that." Although he'd never grown up or visited his grandfather's homeland in Ghana, he knew the seriousness of such a gesture.

"I am showing you utmost respect."

He shook her. "Stop it."

"I want to be with you." Her eyes filled with tears. "I want you back. What do I have to do?"

"Give me time. I'll call you."

HE DIDN'T CALL. He didn't email. He didn't text. She knew it was over. Twice she thought of going by his place but both times she stopped herself. He asked for time and she'd give him all that he needed. She owed him that much. However, when a month passed she prayed to never see him again. She didn't want to see him happy with someone else. Someone who would know how to treat him and remind her of the man she'd lost.

"I can't believe it didn't work out between you two," Tamara said as they shopped for her daughter's birthday. "I thought you'd be perfect."

"You were the only one who thought we'd look good together."

"I didn't say you'd *look* good, I said you'd *be* good."

She snapped her fingers. "Oh that's right I need to get him a "get well" card."

"Why?" Paula asked anxious. "Is he sick? Will he be okay?"

Tamara opened her mouth then closed it and looked at her friend with a smug grin. "I thought you were over him."

"I am."

Tamara just continued grinning.

"What?"

"If you're so interested, why don't you go ask him?"

FOR THREE DAYS Paula debated whether she should go see him or not. Even as she stood at his front door she questioned her decision. But when he opened the door it was too late to turn away. She stared at him. He had his arm in a sling and his leg in a cast. "What happened?"

He shook his head. "You'll only get mad at me?"

"Why would I get mad?"

He bit his lip then sighed. "Because you warned me."

Paula looked at him confused then finally understood. "You ran in flip flops didn't you?"

He nodded. "Tripped down the stairs and sprained my wrist and broke my leg."

"Why are you so clumsy?"

"That's right I'm a big, clumsy baboon. Fortunately, you don't have to worry about that anymore." He closed the door.

Paula stared at it paralyzed. He'd slammed the door

in her face. He didn't want to see her. He had every right. She shouldn't have scolded him. She leaned against the door frame then slid to the ground. She shouldn't have come. He'd rejected her twice. She closed her eyes and hung her head then heard purring. She felt a soft fur brush against her skin. She looked up and saw Wispy. She was no longer a kitten, but was still adorable. She stroked her. "You snuck out, you naughty girl." Paula stood. She'd have to let him know. She rang the bell. He opened it faster than she'd expected as if he'd been waiting by the door.

"What?"

"Wispy got out."

"Oh."

"Who's helping you?"

"I'm managing."

She pushed past him. "Sit down. I brought you some food."

"Paula--."

"I'll leave after you've eaten and you'll never see me again," she said. His place was a mess, which wasn't like him. He had dishes in the sink, clothes on the floor, paper scattered, dust on the plants and shelves. "When was the last time your housekeeper cleaned up?"

"I gave her time off."

"Fine." She'd clean up instead. She prepared his meal, but he refused to let her feed him, so she got to work cleaning up. She tidied the kitchen, washed the dishes, mopped the floor and then vacuumed and dusted his living room and bedroom. She washed his clothes and ironed them then put them away. It was when she was hanging up his shirts that she saw his gray tweed jacket. The one she'd refused to wear when he'd offered it to her. It still had a smudge on the hem. She slipped it on then looked at herself in the full length mirror. She looked ridiculous. It was obviously too large and the color clashed with her complexion, but she didn't care.

At first the realization shocked her. She could hear her mother's voice, feel the sharp sting of the spoon hitting her skin for not being good enough. She remembered the stinging tears of pain of having to pack because the third wife had won. She'd gotten rid of them and her father hadn't fought for them to stay. She remembered on the flight to Canada promising herself that she'd one day be just as powerful as the third wife. She'd be cunning and bold. She'd be beautiful and demand respect. But in her quest to be like the third wife she'd lost herself. She'd lost some of her compassion. She'd become a thin veneer of a woman she'd always hated. No more.

She didn't care what anyone thought. She realized as she looked at herself that Conrad had never been the problem. She'd been afraid of what people would think about her, but not anymore. For the first time in her life other's opinions didn't matter. She didn't care. She smiled at her reflection and hugged herself. All that mattered was that the coat belonged to the man she loved.

She returned to the kitchen humming.

"That jacket's too big for you," Conrad said behind her.

"I know. I like it." She turned to him, her heart pounding. "Actually I love it." She kissed him and this time his kiss wasn't like hot cinnamon chocolate but sweetened blackberries--mouth watering juicy and delicious. And when she drew away the guarded look that had been in his gaze before was gone. In its place was a sense of trust that made her heart soar. There was no chasm between them. He knew he could trust her with his heart. He could trust that she'd always be there for him no matter what anyone thought. That she was proud to be with him and nothing would change that.

Conrad suddenly swore.

"What?"

"I can't even hold you."

She wrapped her arms around him. "That's okay. There's plenty of time for that." She rested her head against his chest and sighed."Your grandmother's not going to like this."

Conrad kissed the top of her head. "She'll get used to the idea."

"I hope so. I have to thank her."

"For what?"

Paula only smiled and hugged Conrad tighter. He was a keeper and she'd never let him go.

ABOUT THE AUTHOR

Dara Girard, an award-winning, national bestselling author of more than forty novels and many short stories, from romance to suspense, loves telling stories.

Born in the US to immigrant parents, Dara enjoys pulling from her Jamaican, British, Nigerian heritage and exposure to various cultures to bring what reviewers and fans call "vivid emotional stories" to life. She is best known for her popular Henson Series, the mysterious Clifton Sisters, and the fun Black Stockings Society.

Visit her website to sign up for her newsletter and get sneak peeks, monthly updates on new releases, and special offers.

For more information visit
www.daragirard.com